The
Grumpy Git's Guide
to Technology

This book is dedicated to Matt, Dirk, JBC, Theo and Isaac,
who have always had answers for some very stupid questions.

First published in the United Kingdom in 2011 by
Portico Books
10 Southcombe Street
London
W14 0RA

An imprint of Anova Books Company Ltd

Illustrations by Damien Weighill

The moral right of the author has been asserted.

ISBN 9781907554407

A CIP catalogue record for this book is available from the British Library.

10 9 8 7 6 5 4 3 2 1

Printed and bound by Everbest Printing Ltd, China.

This book can be ordered direct from the publisher at
www.anovabooks.com

The Grumpy Git's Guide to Technology

Ivor Grump

PORTICO

CONTENTS

Introduction

I've finally worked out why they don't have *Tomorrow's World* on television any more. It would be way too scary. These days we get a great big dose of technology in almost everything we do, such is the pace of innovation and change. When you have automatic checkouts that talk to you, just going to the supermarket can be like an episode of *Tomorrow's World*. So to make itself stand out above the digital tsunami of products available in Maplin or on Amazon, the twenty-first century version of *Tomorrow's World* would have to be quite a radical, science-heavy programme. It would probably be like an Open University lecture, but in colour and with fewer beards.

It was much easier in the past when Howard Stableford would show us a small pill that would be our dinner of the future or Judith Hann would run through the mind-boggling potential of a solar-powered calculator. We got excited about digital stuff back then because it was new and funky. The future was like a David Bowie *Space Oddity* video, we were going to be growing food on the moon and travelling from London to Glasgow on a magnetic induction-powered monorail.

After a while you began to realize that not everything they trailed on the programme was going to make it to the production line. There were quite a few science punts that never came off. On most episodes of *Tomorrow's World* there was at least one item that looked great, made sense, but for some reason or other got stuck in a development cul-de-sac. You'd sit patiently waiting for this new science breakthrough to feed through and it would never come. How disappointed am I that I never got driven to school in my dad's personal hovercraft?

In *iGrump* we take a jaundiced, grumpy journey through many of the things that would have appeared in *Tomorrow's World* in the past, such as the increasingly complicated mobile phone, the increasingly emaciated laptop and the increasingly hot plasma screen. It's not just a rant at people who have iPhones or iPads, though you could easily fill a chapter or two with my views on the kind of people who seize upon each and every new i-item with religious fervour. These i-zealots would have Steve Jobs deified and probably go on a Hajj to Apple HQ in California if they could.

Neither is it an opus on the scale of *I, Claudius*. Although like the Roman emperor Claudius, I, Grump, have no idea how to turn off the voicemail on my mobile phone. (And I've got so many picture texts from Messalina that I can't even open). No, the net is cast far and wide to cover all elements of technology that have imposed themselves on our everyday life, and not just the obvious ones. So you will find subjects like parking the car and football punditry within this book along with the reaffirmation of the need for family values.

Family, I hope you'll agree, is important. When you decide to start a family you don't realize that all those nights spent reading out *Thomas the Tank Engine* and *Postman Pat* are going to be rewarded by your little darlings explaining how digital stuff works in the future.

There was a moment in *The Osbournes* TV series that many natural technophobes like me can relate to. Ozzy is given the remote control to a new state-of-the-art television set. He presses a few buttons to try and switch it on but nothing happens. He aims it at the screen and again nothing happens. He looks at it for a couple of minutes, utterly bewildered by all the buttons and the complexity of the thing. Then he bellows, "Jack!" And his son, Jack Osbourne, comes downstairs and sorts it out. I haven't enjoyed a rockstar's lifestyle of excess fuelled by drugs and alcohol, but I do exactly the same thing. It's so much simpler than reading the manual.

While my children are digital natives, I am a digital immigrant, desperately stumbling around trying to understand as much as I can, but only partially succeeding. I know there are analog fundamentalists out there who cling on to their vinyl records, their typewriters and their film cameras, but it's a losing battle. I have little time for them. I don't object to the digital age, what I object to is the speed at which it is being thrust upon us. It's coming at us so quickly that it's hard to keep up.

I'm happy to report that there are some rare instances where digital technology has been tried and almost universally rejected in favour of old technology. One such example can be found in the music business. My belief that technology was the future, stopped my rock'n'roll career dead in its tracks.

In the early 1980s, when I was still young and impressionable, I really wanted to be a rock'n'roll drummer. I had a whopping £500 saved from a summer job and it was either going to be splashed out on a drum kit or a better car. (Yes, in those days you could get a better car for £500.) Then I saw an item on *Tomorrow's World* that said drum kits were on the way out and in the future all rock music would be powered by drum machines. Ultravox were in the charts, the Human League were in the charts, electro music was on the rise. This was the future sound. So I bought a car and forgi. In this case, I think everyone was a winner.

Ivor Grump

Television

'As Fräulein Maria sang so convincingly in
The Sound of Music, 'nothing comes from nothing,
nothing ever could,' that warm glow from your plasma
screen is a lot of kilowatt hours running through your
electricity meter as the Greenland ice cap melts.'

One Channel Television

Until the arrival of the home computer, your television was the most technological piece of equipment in the house. Kids today have grown up with multi-channel televisions and flat screens, not some creaky old Bakelite box with glowing valves that might give you ITV (yes, that's ITV without a number after it, there was only one) if it felt like it.

I grew up solely watching the BBC. Not because we were very posh, but because my dad got angry with the tuning knob one time and bashed the TV. Thereafter it refused to give us anything but BBC1 (there was a 2 in there somewhere but finding it was like trying to contact Flash Gordon on the other side of Ursa Minor, a lot of Telstar-like whirs and interference).

Those were the days when you could actually bash a bit of technology in the hope that it might fix the problem, TVs being the most picked upon. Those days are long gone. I think we now all accept that bashing a digital camera that has stopped working, or a printer that has stopped printing, isn't going to effect a solution. It may make you feel better and re-establish your superiority over it – yeah, you may be a small black box, but I can dent you – but it's not going to make the gadget feel any better about its role in the world. Digital circuits don't tend to reconnect themselves magically, no matter how hard you stare at them, or how many expletives are vented in their presence.

The TV Space Race

Since the 1950s televisions have undergone a revolution, and while it's great to have colour and more channels, the pace of change is beginning to get ridiculous. I'm all for choice, but not bewildering choice. In the 1950s there was black and white television; in the 1960s we got colour television; in the 1970s we got colour television and Teletext; in the 1980s we got Channel 4, but to make up for the disappointment we also got VHS recorders.

In the 1990s it went M.A.D. mad. We got widescreen televisions that were massive. For the movie fan who hated having his films squashed, you could buy a screen that was a whole 24 inches across. Were Britain's lounges and sitting rooms big enough to hold a TV of those epic proportions? Before some university research project could waste money answering the question, along came the gargantuan 27-inch widescreen to be followed by the behemoth that was the 32-inch screen.

For those who thought that the 32-inch was on the borders of bad taste, these new beasts were something else. They not only had a screen like a cinema, they weighed as much as a cinema. Burglars could sue you for long-term back problems if you didn't put appropriate handles on them. But were the manufacturers satisfied with 32 inches? Of course they weren't. There was a battle to provide the flattest-fronted 32-inch screen, followed by the next move in the space race, a television the size of a Mini, the preposterously large 36-incher.

While all this was happening in the world of conventional telly, Philips and Sony were working on their game-changer: the plasma television. This luxury item got rid of all those nasty, room-filling cathode ray tube gubbins. You could slap it on the wall and watch TV in bed.

All of a sudden, big screen televisions were a chic designer item. They were must-have items and the sizes were eye-watering. A 40-inch plasma screen could set you back £5,000. To the dismay of those who invested early, these prices rapidly came down and sizes went further up: 42-inch, 46-inch, 50-inch, 60-inch and beyond. Plasma got HD, it got trumped by LCD sets, which in turn have been elbowed sideways by LED sets. Now they're advertising 3D TV – where will it end? Pretty soon it'll be cheaper to buy a TV to cover an entire wall than have it painted.

Feeling Remote

Now that you've bought a large, sophisticated television, Samsung, Panasonic, Sony and the likes don't want to under-button you when it comes to the remote control.

Impressive TV equals impressive remote control, doesn't it…?

What is irritating for them is that the human hand can only hold a relatively small object. You get the feeling if the TV engineers had their way, we would be provided with a remote control the size of a cornflakes packet. They are probably all frustrated Boeing 757 cockpit designers and fantasize about the unlimited arrays of buttons and switches they could have in their dream job….

"TV control off standby."

"TV control off standby, check."

"Select Channel One."

"Channel One selected, check."

"Volume control to level five."

"Level five, check."

"White level balance to slight blue positive gain."

"Sorry, Captain, I don't seem to have a button for that. Doh, it's that dream again…"

The engineers when told they can't have a bigger remote control handset, have gone into a giant sulk and said "Oh, all right, I'll make it really small then!" but instead of reducing the number of buttons, have decided to cram all the buttons in they designed, but make them extra-tiny. With only about four or five microns in between each 20-micron button there is no longer the space to write the function of the button, so it's reduced to an acronym like CPR or CLR or PGF and you have to guess what the blazes that means.

Even if you can work out what each button is supposed to do, actually pressing the individual button and not several at once requires extreme concentration and the kind of intense light normally associated with operating theatres and not your lounge environment.

The fact that most people only use a few of the buttons on their remote control seems to have passed manufacturers by. In the new Grump Republic, TVs would come with a simple remote that allowed you to change channels, increase volume, go to the Red Button and little else.

For the techno nerd who wanted a button to vary the screen refresh rate, there would a Boffins' Remote available at extra charge.

Here's What You Can Do With It...

The modern TV remote is so hyper-complicated and button-rich that you probably could land a Boeing 757 using one. They don't look dissimilar from the kind of devices used by model airplane anoraks to land their replica Wellington bombers and their Hawk trainers. However the big problem would come on final approach when things got a bit tense. With such small buttons on the remote you could easily end up jabbing the "retract undercarriage" button when you meant to apply "reverse thrust" and the result would not look pretty. Or inexpensive.

If in Doubt...Press It

There are usually about twenty "What Does That Do?" buttons on every modern remote control. These are buttons with a mystery function. They must do something, they must have a purpose in life, but what that purpose is remains shrouded in mystery. Even when you take your courage in your hands, point the remote and fire, the TV remains unmoved by your infrared exhortation.

If you could find the manual you might stand a better chance, but that disappeared ages ago, and even when you had it you came to the conclusion it had been written by a Vietnamese child and printed in 4-point type.

Ye Olde Days of Remote

There was a time when the remote control was a very exotic piece of equipment. To have your own remote control when they first came out was the mark of a swanky Early Adopter. Not that we knew what early adopters were in those days.

I can remember my friend Mark Evans coming round to my house just so that he could have a go with our TV remote control. It rather spoiled it that we'd seen them being used in American television programmes for the previous 15 years, but the UK finally got them and embraced them. No matter that our lounges were so small, that by the time you'd found it, you could have reached across and changed the channel on the set itself, this was progress, this was living the American way.

It'll be interesting to see what benchmarks of technological innovation our children remember. Depressingly, it's most likely to be "My First Facebook Page".

I can remember our first digital phone, our first TV set which wasn't permanently tuned to BBC1, our first remote, our first electronic tennis game, my first electronic calculator (solar powered!), my first mobile phone and the noise my first mobile phone made when unexpectedly immersed in water. That's also a part of adapting to new technology - knowing which electronic items will survive a slight tumble onto concrete or a short trip into water. So far, not many.

Run Out of Batteries Again

Due to its size and its propensity to be chucked around, dropped, sat on, and wedged places, the TV remote control lives out a pretty unhappy sort of life. Many are scarred, many more are battered. They often go missing. They are the supermarket trolley of the home.

If there were a *Toy Stories*-style animation for household appliances then the TV remote would be voiced over by someone with a manic depressive voice.

Out of sheer spite their batteries give up the ghost three times more quickly than any other battery-driven appliance in the home.

However, they do provide the odd comedy moment. When my 80-year-old father-in-law comes round he seems to have endless fun with it. Being a patient man, he'll try every button in turn to get the channel he wants. He'll study it a while, get his specs out, then press them all, all over again. When that doesn't work he'll fish out a new set of batteries and painstakingly install them. And then repeat the process. At which point my son will breeze past and say "Hello, Grandad" and take the DVD player remote control from him and hand him the one that controls the TV.

That's the problem when you have separate remotes for your Freesat, your TV and your DVD. Sod's law being what it is, the one you need will always have migrated somewhere.

HD Ready

Televisions are always keen to tell you that they're HD Ready. Like the Boy Scouts of the domestic appliance world they are always prepared, always HD Ready. Should a broadcaster try and sneak a high-definition programme onto your screen without warning, then you can be confident that you won't miss a single pixel because your set is HD Ready and is waiting for it.

The phrase makes it sound like HD is still being prepared in the great TV boffins' lab somewhere – we know it's coming, we just don't know when. Except we've had HD for years now but for some reason the TV manufacturers are so beloved of the phrase HD Ready they can't kick the habit. Presumably anxious customers aren't satisfied with the phrase that it's an HD TV, they must keep asking, "but is it HD Ready?"

Wig Finder General

Not only is my television HD Ready, it's HD steady and it's HD go. Seeing people up close in high definition certainly cuts the telegenic wheat from the chaff, I can tell you. I'm sure it's not what Barbra Streisand's been looking forward to. Every time I see her on the box it's like someone's put a massive filter over the lens and she appears courtesy of "New Mistyvision". If you switched on in the middle of the interview you might almost think they had blurred the screen to protect the victims's identity. The clinical high-resolution of HD will take some getting round.

I know *Country File* lost their age discrimination case after firing an older presenter, but generally speaking, providing it's not a former *Big Brother* contestant or a WAG, people prefer to see attractive young flesh on the screen, not a bunch of leathery old turtles. Though I might make an exception for the youngish, fat wine expert on *Saturday Kitchen* who always seems terribly pleased with himself.

HD has also turned me into a terrible wig spotter. Now that F1 is in HD I'm forever staring at former team owner Eddie Jordan's hairline. If it *is* a wig, it's a brilliant one.

Of course, the latest next-big-thing to surpass HD has come along and now we're being exhorted to buy 3D televisions. Friends who have watched 3D football on Sky say it's very good. I'm not going to be finding out in a hurry. My 3D cinema experiences left me feeling like I'd just encountered a Force 11 in the Channel.

TV or Heater?

Plasma televisions are suspiciously cheap these days. Why? I'll tell you why.

The major TV manufacturers are being sponsored by Europe's top energy suppliers. It's a conspiracy to get us to use far more electricity than we did before. Who can resist the lure of big screen entertainment for under £500? You can't, can you? Well, I couldn't. Once you've got your cheap plasma screen installed, your energy consumption takes off like a space shuttle.

Have you ever been close to a plasma screen and felt the heat they chuck off? As Fräulein Maria sang so convincingly in *The Sound of Music,* "nothing comes from nothing, nothing ever could," that warm glow is a lot of kilowatt of hours running through your meter.

Our plasma screen gives off so much heat that we can watch *Ready, Steady, Cook* and barbecue chicken drumsticks in front of it at the same time. I'm not a mean man but I tell the kids it's either the TV or the central heating, you can't have both on at once. Given the choice they tend to opt for the TV, though, I can tell you now, I'd sooner watch the gas-fired boiler for an hour than an episode of *Hollyoaks*.

Freeview, Freesat and Uncle Tom Cobbley

You buy one thing, 15 seconds later you discover if you'd waited just a nadge longer you could have bought the next big thing that everybody's raving about. Sound familiar? Here's a sequence that might be.

They introduce the Freeview Box. Hmm, you think, that might be good, as you don't need Sky, but a few extra channels wouldn't go amiss…

So you buy a Freeview box. Doh!

They only go and launch TVs with built-in Freeview, which means you don't have to have a separate box with a separate remote control, leads, cables and fuss. Your Freeview box maybe senses that you don't have as much love for it as you might and constantly tries hard to impress you with new channels it's "detected" flagged up on screen every time you turn it on. But you're a heartless consumer and when the time comes to renew your television you make your mind up to buy one with built-in Freeview. Doh!

You only find out that the new latest thing is Freesat, where you can buy a Freesat box and a satellite dish and get lots of HD channels along with the Freeview ones you already have.

Hmm, it's too soon to buy a new TV so what the heck, you can't make a mistake this time round, so you buy a Freesat box. Doh!

You only find out that you can now get Freesat HD with a receiver and recorder combined to record all your favourite programmes in high definition. How good would that have been...? And so it goes on.

Catch-Up TV

It's been exactly the same with video recorders. First we had the fight to the death between VHS and Sony Betamax, which VHS won.

There was a brief flurry with the laser disk, like a long-playing record that would play you pre-recorded movies but which sank without trace after its 15 minutes of fame in the video shop window.

Then we had recordable DVDs, followed by re-writable recordable DVDs. Then we had recorders with Hard Disks and Sky Plus. Then we had Blu-ray players, followed by Blu-ray recorders. Parallel to that we have the BBC's iPlayer and ITV and C4's catch-up services, which potentially make them all redundant.

If the online programmes can get over the quality threshold and the buffering issues then why go anywhere else? Right now the resolution is so bad when you view online that it's like watching a television programme through the bottom of an old milk bottle, but if the BBC re-invested the money they waste on their websites then it could be a real rarity. Something the viewers actually want.

'Hello, is that Mr Grump...?'

The voice from Mexico tells me immediately that it's my friends from Acme Media on the line. Every three months they ring me up without fail to tell me that they have a special gift for me – a reward to their loyal customer for using their telephone and broadband package. Naturally, I'm overwhelmed. For me? A special gift? I tell them I feel as lucky as Eeyor on his birthday when he gets a red balloon from Piglet – who accidentally bursts it. This story is listened to with silent incomprehension before they resume the script: "we'd like to offer you our special TV package..."

For a man who could live on a diet of raw cold callers I am exceedingly polite. The reason I don't need any more TV is that with all the catch-up services available there is never enough time to watch the free stuff, let alone pay for more I don't want.

'Would you like a gold HDMI cable with that...?'

Talking about getting sold stuff you don't want, something that really irritates me is salesmen who try and flog you overpriced cables to go with your new TV. It's not enough that they try it on with the dubious extended warranty. When they try that old chestnut the best thing to say is,

"Do you think it's going to break down, then?" To which they can only say no.

When you buy a TV they want to sell you a cable for £30 that you could buy on eBay for a fiver. Now I don't know about you, but I've never watched a movie on DVD and thought, "Hang on, the quality would have been so much better if I'd bought a special gold-plated HDMI cable to stretch between the DVD player and television."

Audio aficionados, who fuss over the slightest hiss and crackle, insist on the best quality cables money can buy. But then again they're the kind of people who iron their socks and wake up in a cold sweat when they remember they filed a Jean-Michel Jarre record under M and not J.

With video cables it either works or it doesn't and you can stuff your expensive cable up your 5-year warranty.

Mr Scart the Socket Maker

Now that I've started using them, I suppose we're going to have to resolve the acronyms issue. Technology is full of them and there's no dodging the subject.

I was rather surprised by a pub quiz question that came up the other day, which was: What does the acronym DVD stand for? Surely that's obvious: Digital Video Disc. It turns out it's not, it's actually Digital Versatile Disc.

I've gaily tossed the phrase HDMI cable into your reading matter yet I can only guess what it stands for. That's not important, though, I know what it looks like and I know the job it does. It links high-techy audio visual things to other high-techy things – games consoles to TVs, camcorders to TVs, DVD players to TVs. Without reference to the Internet

I'm going to plump for High Definition Media Interface. It may or may not be correct; I'm not going to find out. If I knew what all the techy acronyms stood for my wife would divorce me. I'd have to change my name to Ian and spend my days lavishing attention on audio cables and studying the dynamic range of hi-fi speakers.

Television has also given us the SCART socket, which is like an HDMI cable for the 1980s, a time of big hair, big shoulders and big sockets. No idea what the SCART stands for but I'm pretty sure it wasn't invented by Mr Scart.

Television also gave us NICAM digital stereo, which at one point in TV sales was the must-have latest innovation. Who would even bother looking that up? Like the television auto-record feature, it's fallen by the wayside to be replaced by home cinema and other shinier toys.

Camcorders

Now, you might be thinking, "Get over it, Grump, and move on." Cars get better, more reliable, safer, fuel-efficient and so on, yet you don't hanker back to a Morris 1100, even if it was the venue for some Grump firsts. That's true.

Cars evolve, televisions evolve, video recorders evolve and camcorders evolve. The only trouble is all your family memories are then stored on a variety of media dating back to the late 1980s. You might be able to ditch your old VHS movie favourites like *Chitty Chitty Bang Bang* and get them all on Blu-ray, but "Theo's first birthday" from 1992 isn't going to be available on Blu-ray any time soon.

So I'm stuck with family movies on 8mm film (my sister being horrible to me in the 1960s while wearing hysterical ankle socks), 8mm film converted to VHS, VHS tapes, Hi8 tapes (lots of footage of the wife in hilarious baggy jumpers and spotty leggings), miniDV, miniDV HD and now M.peg files on the computer.

Some poor soul, and it's likely to be me, is going to have to convert most of those to digital format so they can be viewed by the Grump dynasty in the future. Because it's a complete pain in the arse to hang on to a cine-projector, a VHS player, an Hi8 player, the miniDV camera, the miniDV HD camera. Plus, transfer the digital files from their computer to back-up DVDs (oh yes, and keep a back-up DVD player to play them on).

This is the big ticking bomb that people are going to have to address. Having stuff on hard disk is not forever. Not only do they fail, they fade out and die. So to be absolutely certain that you've got your life's memories archived, you need multiple hard disks and back-up CDs or DVDs.

Alternatively, you could be like a war artist and just sketch the big events in your life and keep them in a portfolio..

Mobile Phones

'The laughable thing is, people who complain about the effects of radio waves from transmitters two hundred metres away from their house are quite happy to stick a small one right against the side of their head!'

We Used to Wait

The mobile phone is an excellent example of a good piece of technology that's undermining the fabric of our society. We have lost the ability to be patient because we can have things whenever we want them.

When I wanted to buy Norman Greenbaum's single *Spirit in the Sky*, I walked to the shops (on my own, aged 10) and ordered it. The following Saturday I walked back to the record shop and collected it. And I treasured that record. I can still recall the thrill of the Dansette stylus clunking into the groove and the opening instrumental organ bars.

These days if my children hear something they like on the radio it takes them about 25 seconds to download it from Amazon or iTunes. Done. Sorted and probably not treasured.

It's the same with mobile phones. If you want to talk to someone, you can do it straight away, on their mobile phone. And if you can't, then you get irritable and think "Why have they got it switched off?" That should be the creed when you give out your mobile phone number. You sign a pact with the devil – or your phone company – a promise to be on-call whenever you're required.

Mobiles are all part of the instant gratification culture that has grown up, and I'm talking about everything from ready-meals and emails to the very nadir of now, now now-ism: twittering and tweets. I wonder how many Nobel laureates tweet – not many is my guess.

Necessary Evil

Don't get me wrong, I'm not a technology shunner. There are people who gain a lot of pleasure from telling you, "I've never owned a mobile phone and I never will." Or, "I don't own a computer, I wouldn't have one in the house." These people are stupid. Some of them are beyond stupid.

You've broken down in your car in the middle of the countryside at night. What are you going to do, send a carrier pigeon to the AA? In circumstances like that, a mobile phone might be very useful, mightn't it? You could fill 100 books with the stories of people rescued from mountains or cliff tops after contacting the emergency services via their mobile phone. Without it they'd have been contributing to RoSPA statistics. So in a way the mobile phone is a very un-Darwinian tool, it's making the survival instincts of the gene pool a whole lot muddier.

I hate my mobile phone in so many different ways but I know I need it. If only to satisfy my daughter who stands by the front door when I am going away on a trip and demands, "Daddy, have you remembered your mobile phone?" and "are you taking the charger?" and "have you remembered to top it up?" I've normally remembered to do one of the three.

I know I need it. Only a certain select band of people have the number. All the people who have the number I love and so it's always a pleasure to answer it. Oh, and come to think of it, Brittany Ferries have the number as well, but we can work on that one.

A Phone 4 U Comrade

I liked mobile phones a lot more when they were quite primitive, when all you could do was phone people. What I would call a Ronseal arrangement. It was a phone, it was mobile, you could phone people while you were mobile. They should have been sold in tins with that on the side.

Amusingly, Americans call them cell phones and it never ceases to appeal to my childish sense of humour to bate them about it. Whenever I'm talking to an American colleague and they say, "I'm on my cell phone" I give a pantomime intake of breath and sound astounded, "You're in a cell...?!" And they have to explain that no, they're not in a cell with a phone. It's called a cell phone.

You couldn't get away with that level of tomfoolery with a British person, as we don't have an irony bypass.

The earliest phones were best because there were no great features on them. Perhaps it's my inherent begrudging, communist psyche; I liked them best when there was no one-upmanship, when we had the people's phone. Some were a little swankier than others, but the difference between the basic phone and the top of the range was the difference between a Lada Riva and a Lada Riva deluxe.

Now phones have truly become like cars. You can still get a basic model, but the explosion of innovation has been at the top end of the market with phones that offer you HD cameras and movies sent to your phone.

You have to ask yourself, if your life is so boring that you're reduced to watching epic cinematic experiences on a screen three inches by two inches then you deserve the moniker that comes after the word "complete". You must be so desperately dull that a book is beyond you and you have no idea how to fill your time, other than gawping into your lap.

If you do enjoy watching movies on your iPhone 4 then maybe you'd like to look at some of the world's greatest works of art through a telescope. Or how about some of the greatest works of fiction, cut to five paragraphs…?

Camera With Phone Attached

Instead of developing mobile phones that can do tiny, stupid and insubstantial versions of games or films or music that you'd be better off enjoying on a larger scale at home, the manufacturers should be concentrating on the things that really matter. How about designing a battery that powers a phone for two weeks? Why not spend time making phones that have very good reception, so you don't have to wander out into the middle of a B-road to get a signal? Why not make a mobile phone that it is impossible for a child to break?

The reason they don't is because they're not gimmicks and don't add to the specification list by which they're judged against other phones. It would be nice if it could sit on the spec list: camera phone (tick), social networking (tick), not a c**p battery (tick).

When a friend bought a phone with an eight-megapixel camera he was very keen to show it off to me. Eight megapixels is massive. He could do studio work with that.

I asked him to send me some test images so I could compare the quality, at which point he told me he'd only taken four pictures in the three months he'd had it and they were still on the phone. Yet he bitches like Elton when his battery runs out.

Mobiles in the Grump Republic

The sum total of all this indulgence in mobile phone features is that in 20 or 30 years' time orthopaedic surgeons are going to be having a field day. So many people will have problems in their cervical vertebrae that they will name a syndrome after it. We had RSI (Repetitive Strain Injury) for workers who constantly use a computer mouse; soon we're going to get MPN (Mobile Phone Neck) caused by constantly having your neck bent over and looking down at Angry Birds or whatever the latest game is.

Anyone who gets MPN in the new Grump Republic will automatically have their phone replaced with a Mobile Phone Lite until they're better. This phone can make and receive calls, you can text and that's it. There will be no voicemail, just an outgoing message saying, "I'm doing something far too important to answer a phone call", calculated to whittle down the number of callers.

It's the message I put on when I'm out of the office.

Signalling, a Change

Rather than increase the density of transmitters, it would be so much easier if the mobile phone makers gave us phones that were more sensitive to received signals. Admittedly, it is funny seeing people wander round in a haphazard fashion in order to get a signal on their phone. The builders vaguely working on our extension have found that the ideal spot to make a call is in the middle of the road 20 metres below our house. This involves a fair degree of jeopardy, but such is their addiction to the mobile phone they're prepared to try.

It makes you wonder how anything got built before we had the mobile phone…

Radio masts are a sensitive issue. The moment anyone applies for planning permission to erect one it's like H.G. Wells' *The War of the Worlds*, "what are these infernal alien machines marching across our landscape?" This NIMBY attitude might be okay if the objectors didn't use mobile phones themselves, but they all do. So, to keep them happy it would be much better if phones could have their range extended.

The laughable thing is, people who complain about the effects of radio waves from transmitters 100 metres away are quite happy to stick a small one right against the side of their head from 0.0 metres away. Such is life.

It's a Hotspot, Dude

The same profound misunderstanding about radio waves applies to radiation. Some parts of the British Isles are a lot more radioactive than others. If you're living in a location that sits on top of sedimentary rocks you're not going to have a high background radiation. But if there are igneous rocks below the ground, such as granite, which emits radon gas, then the dosage is going to be high. People think fondly of retiring to Cornwall but it's where you'll get a lot more background radiation than chalky old Eastbourne.

Think of all those hippy surf dudes heading for Fistral Beach in Newquay. They used to have smiley stickers on the backs of their 2CVs and VW Combis that said 'Nuclear Power? No Thanks'. Cornwall is not only a surf hotspot, it's a radiation hotspot, too. How uncool is that…Dude?

Battery Life Not Included

The extended life of batteries is another sore point for me. I tend to get phones where the display reads three bars, two bars…and no bars. Instantly the warning signal that the battery is low appears, which is enough to exhaust the poor love, after which it immediately retires to its day bed.

The result is that I think I've got lots of battery, then I've got no battery at all.

Even if they're not prepared to have a go at seriously extending the life of their batteries, phone companies could at least produce a more sophisticated power gauge that told you precisely where you stood.

For Pay-As-You-Go customers they can tell you your credit balance to the nearest one pence instantly; they should also be able to tell you how many minutes of phone you've got left. Video cameras have been doing that quite accurately for some time and are able to adjust their prognosis based on whether you're using the foldout screen or the viewfinder. Maybe Mr Ericsson should have a word with Mr Sony.

Ringtones

The one ring tone that everyone knows, even if they can't name it, is the Nokia Tune. It's a Nokia sound trademark now. It's the ring tone from the famously unfunny Dom Jolly sketch where he'd carry around a massive mobile phone. Titter. And then bellow "Hello!" into it after the ringtone. Hilarious.

I'm sure some trendy Arts Council-funded painter dabbling in freeform sheep excrement with a workshop near

Hoxton Square would use it on their phone today ironically. The trouble is, old people have still got it on their phones as their default ringtone, thus ruining all the ironic fun.

Ringtones in an Open-Plan Office

Generally speaking, we've become a bit more sophisticated about the ringtones we choose since the early days of the Crazy Frog. "What does my ringtone say about me?" most people are savvy enough to ask themselves. If you're a middle-aged bloke working in the City and your phone explodes into life on the packed 17:42 service from London Cannon Street to Sevenoaks, and it's a Kylie track, you'd want to answer it pretty swiftly.

I work in a large open-plan office, where the open Savannah of desks reverberates with various ringtones throughout the day. Most are pleasant and distinctive, but there's one shocker: a country and western instrumental medley.

One of the rules when selecting a ringtone should be this: would you be happy exposing your colleagues to it for two whole minutes? Now, normally the girl whose phone it is manages to switch it off before we get to the banjo part, but one day she disappeared for a very long meeting and forgot to take her phone with her.

Our office became like the theme park "Dollywood" for the next 15 minutes, after which someone stapled it inside three Jiffy bags and shoved it in her drawer.

The Grumptones

One indication of how few people ring me is that I can't actually identify my own ringtone. My colleague David, who sits next to me, once leant over and told me my phone was ringing. I listened to the ring tone, which was very pleasant, a bit like 60s elevator music in a Burt Bacharach kind of way. Old but groovy. I said no, it wasn't mine.

"Well," he explained patiently, "it's coming from your bag."

It was, of course, mine.

Texting

Texting and GPS location are probably the two best additions to the mobile phone's core skill. (Unless you're receiving a text sent to your landline and you get an automated voice so incomprehensible that it might not even be English.)

For me, though, writing texts has been the most singularly frustrating thing in the techno world and quite seriously I have come within a gnat's whisker of hurling my phone off the back of a ferry.

My previous phone was not intuitive. In fact, it was wilfully misleading. The delete button and the save-to-drafts button were side by side and I'd get so far into the text only for it to disappear into drafts, then somehow disappear altogether.

What was worse, there was no apostrophe. Call me old-fashioned but I refuse to shorten words and I won't send anything that isn't punctuated properly. I would spend hours searching for the apostrophe on that phone. In the end I handed it over to my children and they couldn't find it.

On one occasion I attempted to send an angry text to my builder. I was sitting at the back of a ferry sailing away from Caen/Ouistreham and I wrote a long, indignant two-page text. It took me 20 minutes to compose and I had to review it carefully to make sure I got the tone right. It was a pithy work of art. Then I decided to change the word "want" to "require", pressed the delete button twice by accident and the whole b******ing thing disappeared! What's more, I knew by the time I re-typed it all, we'd be out of signal range from the coast, thanks to my sodding useless phone. The English Channel beckoned but I held on. It ultimately met its fate on a beach in Corfu and I was never so happy to lose a phone.

This Time It'll Be Better

The next time I bought a phone, I specifically asked the guy from a leading chain of mobile phone shops (the guys in Phones 4u were busy) if it had a proper touchscreen keyboard like the iPhone. He said yes. I bought it. It didn't.

Instead, it had the conventional layout (ABC – DEF – GHI – JKL – MNO etc.) but it was a touchscreen. I couldn't be arsed to take it back. After all, I now had my very first apostrophe.

A Touch Too Much

It frustrates me now because the touchscreen element is so poor that when I press anywhere near the boundary between JKL and TUV it will opt for JKL, which drives me to distraction. And if you think that I'm annoyed, it completely hacks off the predictive text engine, which goes looking for

Polish words that I might be trying to use. In fact, come to think of it, my texts might make a lot more sense in Polish or Croatian these days.

Another element that makes me want to get Basil Fawlty-esque with my phone and give it a damned good thrashing is its tendency to switch to screens because it feels like it. For instance, when I'm trying to top up my phone, the patronising lady at the other end who thinks I have special needs, asks me to press 1 for payment options.

The phone is having none of that. The phone has already switched itself away from the keyboard page to give me a different display I hadn't asked for. So there is no. 1 to be pressed. By the time I've frantically jabbed at every button on the phone twice and got the keyboard display back she's giving me the impatient: "I didn't catch that option" routine, her voice barely able to conceal an attitude of what-am-I-doing-talking-to-this-dimwit. Then I go to press the number 1 as advised and the screen has locked itself. For security reasons, to unlock it I have to draw a finger shape on the touchscreen that I have no recollection of ever doing in that honeymoon phase of ownership when I thought, "this time it's going to be different".

Why anyone should covet my phone, the Zoomty Hey! model (not its real name for legal reasons, but it's just as embarrassing a concoction of words), enough to nick it is beyond me. I'd happily give it away.

Spam Texts

Do you get spam text messages? Spam emails I can understand but spam texts are more worrying. I got one today asking me to forward my accidents details so I could make a claim. I haven't had an accident, so it was obviously a scam. It was sketchy and vague, like one of those bland emails you get from "Sue" who simply says "Hi". Or "Kelly" who says "About tomorrow".

Because so few people actually know my mobile phone number I get a bit Miss Marple about texts like this. Where did they get my number? Was it just a random guess?

Part of the reason for not filling in my mobile number on every online form – apart from the fact that I can't remember it – is that it will oblige me to check it regularly, have it switched on, and recharge it. Like a pet you don't really want but are obliged to maintain until it pops its clogs.

Ear Devices

I'm sorry but I can't take anyone wearing one of these seriously. Unless they're a CIA officer protecting the president. That's where we saw them first and that's where they should stay.

These days you'll see them being worn by minicab drivers and the like, which is so astonishingly dangerous I'm surprised that the police haven't stepped in. I'm sure if it was a food-related issue Jamie Oliver would have done a series on it by now.

It's a well-known fact that men can't multi-task, and driving a car while receiving a set of instructions is definitely two things. Given the road awareness of most minicab drivers, having one thing to do is already pushing the upper boundary of the skills envelope.

I'm quite happy for women to wear them because they can multi-task, but the ladies will always want two that are matching.

Hands Free, Brain Occupied

Now you might say a "hands free" device has exactly the same distracting effect on someone driving a car as an earpiece. This is true. Your ability to drive and concentrate on a phone conversation depends on lots of factors, such as when and where you take the call. It also has a lot to do with the nature of the information you have to compute.

Think of it like a computer's Random Access Memory, or RAM. For instance, if you're driving down the motorway, unless it's in thick fog that has you gripping the steering wheel, you're using up 10 per cent of your computing ability. That allows you to devote 90 per cent of your active grey matter (70 per cent if you're a politician, 50 per cent if you're a front bench spokesman) to a phone conversation about the intricacies of the universe, or for you to deliver precise instructions as to where you left the Superglue remover.

If you're driving a familiar suburban route, then there are a few hazards to watch out for, such as stray dogs, children and Lycra-clad bike riders reinventing the Highway Code to suit themselves. That's going to take 40 per cent of your cerebral RAM, so any phone conversation needs to be of a fairly lightweight and cursory nature.

But if you're driving on an unfamiliar road, trying to work out which turning you need, scanning the ends of roads to find street names, then that will take 95 per cent of your attention and you don't need to be taking a phone call.

And that's what minicab drivers do all the time.

Licence to Ramble

The widespread adoption of the earpiece phone has been an absolute boon to nutters.

Nutters have managed to slip into the mainstream of society, safe in the knowledge that they are no longer as conspicuous. When you used to see someone walking down the street rambling on to themselves, or they were sitting on the back of the bus having an argument with the window, you knew straight away. Nutter.

Now, whenever you see someone talking to themselves, 99 per cent of the time they'll be speaking into some form of hands-free mobile device. Nutters, if they wanted to, could slip entirely under the radar by purchasing an earpiece and not even switching it on. In reality, they are more likely to buy a four-pack of Special Brew and sit on a bench somewhere, but the opportunity is there.

Losing It

One of the big drawbacks of having your life on your phone is what happens when you lose it. Breaking the thing can be bad enough, but the consequences of leaving it on the train or getting it stolen can be devastating.

The Filofax has long gone west. I've still got one, of course, but you'd expect that of me.

All your phone numbers are on it; there'll be dates logged, photos you haven't downloaded, music that needs to be re-installed, epic movies that you still haven't squinted at. And if you've got a smartphone, it isn't so smart now because you have to buy your "apps" all over again.

Then you have to go about the business of informing all your friends and colleagues that you have a new mobile number, but you don't have their numbers to tell them. Ah, modern life.

ParkNav

The consequences of losing your phone will get more severe in the future because the mobile will increasingly be used as a payment device. It's already taking the need to pay with cash out of the parking system. Instead of thrusting a load of coins into a ticket machine – and for a day's parking in London you need the cash float of a small supermarket – you buy time in a numbered parking bay by phoning in your details. It's a marvellous system, while your phone is powered.

Technology is coming to the parking system in another way that could involve your phone but will probably rope in the SatNav. (Those of you discerning enough to buy *The Grumpy Driver's Handbook* will know that I haven't got a bad word to say about SatNavs. So if you're waiting for a diatribe about the outrageous perils of Jane and her SatNav instructions, you're going to be disappointed.)

Cities in the States are installing sensors underneath their parking spots. These sensors tell a central computer if there's a vehicle parked there or not. In the future when drivers are coming into a city, they'll be able to hook up their SatNav to the parking computer and it will direct them to the nearest free spot. How good is that? It will probably work with a GPS-equipped smartphone, too.

The New Rock'n'Roll

The parking app is an example of mobile phone technology at its very best. My son has an app on his phone that displays a pint of lager on the screen, and when you tip the phone, the level of lager changes to match the angle of the phone. Yeah, you get the idea, some are a load of old toot.

Apps are the new rock'n'roll. For every worthy and genuinely useful application there are ten that are trivial nonsense or just a scaled down version of a far better thing.

There are apps that let you know if there are "like-minded" people are in your area. If you're cruising for gay or straight sex, there are many apps that will facilitate your search (I'm told).

Should you want to meet up with people who also like apps, then there's an app for that. If you have sufficient communication skills (and that's a big if), you can arrange to meet at the pub, and…erm…show off your apps.

Most apps are just gimmicks to keep you amused down the pub. The Apple iPhone had the market sewn up for a long while, but then their rivals banded together and struck back with the Android operating system, allowing Samsung, HTC, Sony-Ericsson and LG to compete.

App Challenge

The Gadget Show did a hysterical "app challenge" where two of their presenters were given a series of challenges to demonstrate the strengths and weaknesses of two smartphones and their associated apps. They started off in the centre of Birmingham where they were given an invitation to a formal event that was taking place, except the invite they got was in Spanish!

First they had to translate the email using a translation app, then they had to send it to a printer using a Wi-Fi app, then they had to be directed to a formal dress hire shop using a directory app, then go to the venue using a SatNav app. I don't know about you, but barely a day goes past when I don't get invited to a last-minute formal event in a foreign language for which I have no means of printing out the invitation. Our house is stacked up with boxes of Ferrero Rocher, just waiting.

What was also laughable – and my entire point about this malarkey – was that one of the smartphones ran out of battery before the challenge was through. The *Top Gear* crew, from whom this TV challenge technique seems to have been copied, are sensible enough to play it for laughs. *The Gadget Show* doesn't have that sense of mocking self-irony. They really do believe this stuff is important. What is most worrying is that children will see programmes like this and think this is the stuff of life, rather than what it is in the most part: a vacuous diversion.

'I Can't Be Doing With...'

The whole antipathy towards complex mobile phones is a symptom of a wider view about technology. That it comes on us too fast, in too many different areas and the pace of change is accelerating so fast that we'll never catch up. Faced with several technology mountains to climb, the easiest thing is to throw up your hands in horror and say not for me. Or pretend you can get by without it. People who say, "I can't be doing with mobile phones" could really be doing with mobile phones if they had an easy way in. A less frightening piece of kit, maybe with some wood panelling involved. It would really help old people if there were a Roberts Radio version of the mobile phone. In fact there should be a Roberts Radio version of all technology. The Grump Republic would make it happen. There would be a Roberts Radio microwave, a Roberts Radio MP3 player that resembled an old record player (but considerably smaller and flatter), there would be a Roberts Radio digital camera in the shape of an old twin lens reflex camera and a Roberts Radio camcorder with all the gubbins shoved into an 8mm cine camera casing, circa the time Abraham Zapruder was filming on Dealey Plaza.

Roberts – By Grumpy Appointment

The Roberts Radio SatNav would be voiced by Terry Thomas and would be incredibly polite, full of old school charm. When you missed your intended turning instead of asking you to make a U-turn it would inform you in chummy tones, "I say old boy, I think you just drove past your turning. Would you mind awfully spinning the old gal round and having another try?"

At the end of your journey there wouldn't be the prosaic, "You have reached your destination", the tone would be celebratory. "Dashed well done, old boy. You're here, you're jolly well here. Go and have a pint and a smoke on me."

Where's the Handbook?

Something that always adds to frustration and technophobia is the lack of a proper handbook. Mobile phone manufacturers are just as guilty as all the other techno gadget providers in that they don't supply you with a comprehensive manual.

Costs have to be cut and it seems the first thing to go is a thorough and well-written guide to any expensive bit of kit you've just bought. All those pages, all that shipping, they'd far sooner direct you to a download-able pdf or an online manual. Which can be a lot of fun when it's your computer that's gone wrong and you can't access the blinking manual!

Sent From My iGrump

What is it about the iPhone that makes sane people go ga-ga? In the early days of the iPhone you'd hear new owners waxing lyrical about them with the kind of enthusiasm that bordered on religious fervour. As comedian Marcus Brigstocke once said about iPhone owners, "Look, you just bought one, you didn't invent the thing!".

The wife is a big fan. Probably because she didn't pay for it. What I can't get over is that I splashed out all that money and she still can't hear the blinking ringtone! If I had my way it would be the kind of deep resonant bellow that ships use in fog. Instead it's more like a dog whistle. "Oh, did you ring me?" is the surprised question I get when she looks at the phone and sees six missed calls.

Apple came up with one of the simplest marketing ploys in the email facility that is attached to the phone, which adds the remark at the bottom: "Sent from my iPhone." A day after the launch of the much-coveted iPad in 2010 I got an email from a friend, which appeared to go one better: "Sent from my iPad."

I rang him up and accused him of being a flash bastard to which he laughed and replied he hadn't got an iPad, he just typed that at the bottom of his email. Everyone believed him.

Other iProducts Are Available

iBin – Only allows you to dump the things it feels you should dump.

iBus – Offers fewer seats, higher fares and shorter routes, but, wow, what a cool-looking bus.

iCake – Less icing, less cake and more expensive, but it slices itself up for you.

iGrump… therefore I am.

iPhones – A West Country saying indicating that the person regularly communicates.

iPods – Internet-savvy dolphins.

A Real Turn-Off

They may be a godsend, but they can also be the cause of great social embarrassment. Especially when you forget to turn them off in the theatre. In some situations it's not too bad. For opera and ballet, a ringing phone will probably help break the tedium and at the same time wake a few people up, so not too much harm done there.

In the serious theatre, though, where actors work so hard to create an intense atmosphere and build an illusion, a ringing phone can spoil everything. Actor Richard Griffiths has been known to stop the play and harangue the hapless members of the audience over their ringing phones. Bravo, sir!

Another situation is when your mobile phone decides to ring somebody of its own accord. I cycle to work and my mobile is forever jumping around in the carrier trying to decide which one of my six contacts it should ring. This isn't embarrassing, just expensive. What's embarrassing is when someone rings you up to tell you that they can't make the barbecue you've prepared for them. Then their phone rings you up accidentally from their pocket 10 minutes later and you can hear them talking in the background and you realise that the excuse they've just given is a complete fabrication. That was the end of a great friendship.

Then there's that great big hole you dig for yourself – the bitchy text you send about someone... which you accidentally send to that person. That's always a laugh. That goes hand in hand with the angry email you send on to a friend or colleague as a result of you receiving some piece of tosh in your inbox. You know something on the lines of "Can you believe this piece of c*** I've just been sent." After which you discover you didn't Forward, you Replied and you sent the email to your nemesis.

Finally, there's Compulsive Phone Checking Disorder, the person who comes to dinner with his (it's never socially sensitive women) Blackberry who has to check it every five minutes. "It's no worse than popping out for a fag" is not a defence. You can make guests like this really uncomfortable by offering them your children's Nintendo DS to play, "if you're finding the conversation boring".

The Dangers of Surfing Abroad

One of the drawbacks of having a smartphone is that they are operated by simpletons. A story that regularly hits the news these days runs along the lines of 'Businessman Stunned by £6,000 Phone Bill'. Basically people with Internet-equipped phones go abroad and forget to turn their Data Roaming off. They forget that browsing the Internet at home may cost next to nothing on their cleverly worked out package, but when they go abroad, it costs an arm and a leg. Three legs, actually. It's like buying coffee; you don't think about the cost of a coffee from a vending machine, only if you've got the right coins. You would NEVER sit down for a coffee on the piazza in St. Mark's Square, Venice.

These stupid numpties then appear in a photo holding up their phone bill or their mobile phone in outrage/anguish. I have no sympathy for them at all. If they've gone abroad, then 100% of them will have had to fill empty hours waiting for cabs, planes, trains etc. and could have used a valuable two minutes checking their terms and conditions. Or even reading the texts that are sent to them saying they've used up half their data roaming allowance in the first 30 minutes abroad!

Text and Chatroom Acronyms

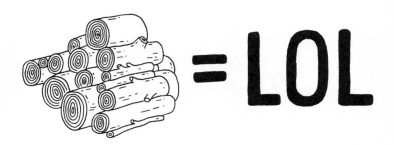 **= LOL**

'There should be no equivocation, LOL equals
Laugh Out Loud, nothing else. It doesn't mean Lots
Of Love, or Leave Off Lass or Leg Over Lately?'

Now, this is where I get a bit schizophrenic. As U know, I will not shorten words on a text message and I view those who do with complete and utter disdain. I also hate people who constantly speak in clichés and insert acronyms and abbreviations into sentences at the drop of a syllable. But the thing is… the other day I caught myself writing something along the lines of, "Can you send it to me ASAP." And I thought, hang on, you great big hypocrite, Grump – you're a word shortener. What would Lynne Truss and Stephen Fry think of you now…?

This started a wave of almost Wittgenstein-ian introspection. Well, for a good 10 minutes anyway. What else did I use without realising it? The obvious one is "OK", short for okay, though nobody is entirely sure what the shortened words are – the embarrassing explanation is that future American president Andrew Jackson couldn't actually spell All Correct and being from Tennessee in the deep South thought it was Oll Korrect.

I wouldn't hesitate to drop FAQ into a sentence – a trio of letters that have risen to great prominence through the rise of the Internet, and I'd probably use AKA without giving it a second thought. I'm not averse to a bit of PYO in the summer, especially if it's strawberries, and which male above the age of 25 isn't required to do a bit of DIY at the weekend?

It's funny, the more you think about it, the more they come sailing out of the woodwork. The cat's just gone AWOL – we'll have to put an APB out on it.

Now the thing about acronyms is that you have to be sure that your acronym means the same thing to the person you're communicating with. For instance, if you email someone that you're going to contact the AA, is it the Automobile Association, Alcoholics Anonymous, American

Airlines, the Athletics Association, Alzheimer's Association, an African American or did you make a mistake and need a new battery? Or want a very small bra?

As you would expect, context is everything. If your car broke down and needed to be recovered it's no use at all contacting Alcoholics Anonymous, even if it was driving you to drink. But what if you don't have that context, as in one of those throwaway phrases added to the end of an exchange. LOL normally means Laugh Out Loud, but some people use it as Lots Of Love. That might make a simple conversation very complicated.

Some AAs (Approved Acronyms) and BAs (Banned Acronyms)

At the onset of the First Grump Republic there would be guidance given as to what was an appropriate acronym and what was considered plain lazy. Please take note, as Internet Service Providers will be tasked with monitoring usage (that's after we stopped them lying about their connection speeds).

AAMOF (As A Matter Of Fact)
Banned. Get off your high horse.

ADAD (Another Day, Another Dollar)
Banned. Platitudinous rubbish.

AFAIK (As Far As I Know)
Banned. This doesn't pass the shortening test. Acronyms must save more typing than this.

AKA (Also Known As)
Approved.

ASAP (As Soon As Possible)
Approved.

ATM (At The Moment)
Banned. We have the word "now" for this. It could also be confused with what the Americans call a cash dispenser. You know, a CD.

ATYS (Anything You Say)
Banned. Acronyms are not to be used for getting sarky.

AWA (As Well As)
Banned. We have the word "also" for this.

B4N (Bye For Now)
Banned. Partings should be such sweet sorrows and a little bit more personal than three lazy digits.

BBS (Be Back Soon)
Banned. I've never liked any of the songs from *Oliver*. It's not as trite as *Who Will Buy This Wonderful Morning* – or whatever that song's official title is.

BCNU (Be Seein' You)
Banned. This is awful on All Kinds Of Levels.
(Yes, AKOL!)

BFF (Best Friends Forever)
Approved. I'm sure my daughter uses this on Facebook

all the time and I really don't want to be given a hard time over it.

BMG (Be My Guest)
Banned. It's the name of a record company.

BTDT (Been There Done That)
Approved. From 17 characters to four characters is a good shortening ratio in anyone's book.

BTW (By The Way)
Approved. Only just, though.

CSL (Can't Stop Laughing)
Banned. See a doctor and get them to change the level of your medication.

CUL or **CUL8R** (See You Later)
Banned. You knew this was never going to get in, didn't you? This is B4N by the back door.

CUZ (Because)
Banned. Oh, please! The last time I saw this word written out it was on a Slade single in the 1970s.

CWOT (Complete Waste Of Time)
Approved. This is very "on message" for the Grump Republic. Although that phrase, "on message" wouldn't survive.

DQMOT (Don't Quote Me On This)
Approved.

DUCWIM (Do You See What I Mean?)
Approved. I quite fancy the idea of adding DUCWIM to a message.

DWBH (Don't Worry, Be Happy :O)
Approved. Though if you want to use an emoticon you have to prove that you are under 18 or have an IQ of less than 50.

EOD (End Of Discussion)
Banned. Pompous git.

EOM (End Of Message)
Banned. You know when the message ends because there are no words there. That's the beauty of empty space.

F2F (Face To Face)
Banned. This never happens in the cyber world, unless it's some dodgy adult in a teenage chatroom, so definitely banned.

F2T (Free To Talk?)
Banned. If you can't even be bothered to type stuff out in full then you're hardly going to be capable of a full conversation, unless you simply mutter acronyms! LOL!

FCOL (For Crying Out Loud)
Banned. Homer Simpson's trademark "Doh!" will do nicely instead.

FOAF (Friend Of A Friend)
Approved. Another great one to add to DUCWIM

FOFL (Falling On The Floor Laughing)
Banned. You can have LOL and ROFL (see page 59),
but FOFL is one too many.

FUBAR (Fouled Up Beyond All Recognition)
Banned. This is simply someone trying to re-invent
SNAFU, which has been around so long it's almost
Chaucerian.

FWIW (For What It's Worth)
Approved.

FYEO (For Your Eyes Only)
Approved.

FYI (For Your Information)
Approved. You see, this is another one I hadn't thought
about. I use this at least twice a week without thinking.
They're creeping up on me. This is getting to be a bit like
a zombie movie. You didn't realise it, but those two
green hands you've been using to type, they're not from
an excess of gardening…

G2G (Got To Go)
Banned.

GAL (Get A Life)
Banned. This kind of insult shouldn't be hurried, it should
be savoured and enjoyed and written out in full. "Get a
life" itself is an abbreviation of a proper insult.

GF (Girlfriend)
Banned. This could mean good friend.

GJ (Good Job)
Approved.

GR8 (Great)
Banned. Three characters from five is disgracefully inefficient.

GTG (Got To Go)
Banned. Ditto.

H8 (Hate)
Banned. Ditto.

HAGN (Have A Good Night)
Banned. See HAND.

HAK (Hugs And Kisses)
Approved.

HAND (Have A Nice Day)
Banned. This is something you say out loud, a supposedly sincere phrase used as a parting gesture. If you're going to reduce it to an acronym you might as well embellish it and say something substantial. We can use a traditional phrase here like MTWBAAYB or MTSSWUYF. That's a bit better don't you think...? Full of warm Celtic charm. May The Wind Be Always At Your Back or May The Sun Shine Warm Upon Your Face.

HHIS (Hanging Head In Shame)
Approved. Just.

HOAS (Hold On A Second)
Banned. Use "Hang on".

HTH (Hope This Helps)
Approved.

IAE (In Any Event)
Banned. This sounds like it should be something to do with the International Atomic Energy commission.

IDC (I Don't Care)
Banned. We Don't Care Either. WDCE.

IDK (I Don't Know)
Banned. IDK-Y.

IIRC (If I Remember Correctly)
Banned. More pomposity.

ILY (I Love You)
Banned. Because if you did then you'd probably devote more time than it takes to make three poxy keystrokes.

IMHO (In My Humble Opinion)
Banned. People who say this really don't have a humble opinion, they have a very grand opinion they want to dress up with some token humility. They might as well save the blather of that letter "H" and use IMO.

IMLTHO (In My Less Than Humble Opinion)
Approved. This is the truth of it.

IMO (In My Opinion)
Approved.

IMPOV (In My Point Of View)
Banned. Banned and triple banned. It should be FMPOV!
This is what happens when non-English speakers get
into chatrooms. The havoc they can wreak. Like in the
Eurovision song contest when other nations are allowed
to sing in English. All of a sudden they think they own
it. My view is this: If you're not going to vote for
Royaume-Uni you can't sing in our language. FMPOV
doesn't exist but I would prefer the West Country
version anyway: FWIS – From Where I Sits.

IOW (In Other Words)
Banned. This is the Isle of Wight.

IRL (In Real Life)
Banned. This is the Republic of Ireland.

JK (Just Kidding)
Banned. This is "Rowling" or "from Jamiroquai".

JTLYK (Just To Let You Know)
Banned.

KIS (Keep It Simple)
Approved. As is KISS, used when people are addressing
me in direct terms i.e. Keep It Simple, Stupid. It's not

listed here but I'd like to see KMA widely adopted – as in Kiss My Aunt.

KIT (Keep In Touch)
Banned. What's the point of keeping in touch if you're only going to be bombarded by a load of acronyms? FWIW.

KWIM (Know What I Mean?)
Approved. So approved.

L8R (Later)
Banned. Any kind of acronym that has a figure in the middle makes it look like a nightclub owner's personalised number plate.

LMIRL (Let's Meet In Real Life)
Banned. You're bound to be disappointed. It's much better to continue the illusion that your correspondent is cool and trendy, not the kind of person to combine socks and sandals with unsuitable shorts of the kind that Ivan Lendl wore when playing Wimbledon in the 1980s.

LMAO (Laughing My A** Off)
Approved.

LOL (Laughing Out Loud)
Approved.

LTNS (Long Time No See)
Banned. Is it any surprise that it's been a long time when all you do is talk in letters?

MMB (Message Me Back)
Approved.

MOS (Mom Over Shoulder)
Banned. Parent abuse shouldn't be tolerated in any form.

MTFBWU (May The Force Be With You)
Banned. *Star Wars* geek.

NALOPKT (Not A Lot Of People Know That)
Approved. Presumably the Michael Caine companion
to YOSTBTBDO! from *The Italian Job*. Though it might
be difficult fitting it into an Internet conversation.

NOYB (None Of Your Business)
Approved.

NRN (No Response Necessary)
Approved.

OMG! (Oh My Goodness! Or, Oh My God! Or, if you're
ecclesiastical, Oh My Grace!)
Approved.

OTTOMH (Off The Top Of My Head)
Approved.

OWTTE (Or Words To That Effect)
Banned. You clearly can't be bothered to use whole
words in the first place.

PCM (Please Call Me)

Banned. If you're going to oblige someone to go through the bothersome business of actually making a phone call and doing that awkward direct communication thing, then you can at least spell it out.

POV (Point Of View)

Approved.

ROFL (Rolling On the Floor Laughing)

Approved. IMHO this book is one long ROFL from start to finish.

RSN (Real Soon Now)

Banned. You really do need to use gooderer English than this.

SFETE (Smiling From Ear To Ear)

Banned. This reeks of someone dreaming up their own acronym and hoping that the world adopts it. We have LOL, ROFL and LMAO to express mirth.

SIT (Stay In Touch)

Banned. Anyone who lived through the Barbara Woodhouse years would understand why this should never be used as an acronym.

SITD (Still In The Dark)

Approved. My usual state.

SOH (Sense Of Humour)

Approved. This is an acronym from the personal columns normally preceded by the letter "G". But are there any other kinds of SOH that people like to advertise? SSOH wouldn't be much of a draw (Sick). Neither would CSOH (Childish). And people are very poor judges of their own SOH. I once interviewed someone who professed himself, in a complete deadpan, to be "tremendous fun". I imagined they would only be tremendous fun to a bored grizzly bear who found them in their cave.

SUP (What's Up?)

Banned. This is also the acronym for Stand Up Paddleboarding – you know, like a surfboard that you can paddle about on flat water. Something to make you look young and virile when you have it on the roof rack.

TBC (To Be Continued)

Banned. You see I would imagine TBC as To Be Confirmed. Surely that has far more mileage than To Be Continued…?

TGIF (Thank Goodness It's Friday)

Banned. Slacker.

TIA (Thanks In Advance)

Banned. As with ILY, if someone is deserving of thanks, then they're deserving of more than three measly keystrokes.

TMB (Text Me Back)

Approved. Though I'm not sure why you would
need the "B".

TMI (Too Much Information)

Approved.

TOY (Thinking Of You)

Banned. Where's the poetry gone in how we talk to each
other? I don't regularly quote sonnets to Mrs Grump,
even if she is more temperate than a summer's day, but
surely someone who is in our thoughts is worthy of
more than the distilled emotion of three letters. Should
I add TOY to a text to Mrs Grump I would probably get
a caustic UYB in response. And talking of UYB...

VPL (Visible Panty Line)

Approved.

WFM (Works For Me)

Approved. WFM2.

WTG (Way To Go)

Banned. This is a useless Americanism. Don't get me
wrong, I'm not averse to our transatlantic cousins
enriching our language (except when they convert nouns
to verbs, such as "to summit" a mountain). I love
"Doh!", I love "Meh" (which is like a shortened version
of "so what, couldn't really care less"), but Way To Go
is CWALP (CodsWALloP)!

WTH (What The Hell?)
Banned. What's wrong with re-introducing some
of the good old words and phrases of P.G. Wodehouse?
These can be almost as succinct. How about "Cripes!"

WYRN (What's Your Real Name?)
Banned. See LMIRL.

WYSIWYG (What You See Is What You Get)
Approved.

XOXO ("Hugs and Kisses")
Approved. This is also the third most popular boys'
name in China.

YRG (You aRe Good)
Banned. TH or Top Hole is how we will express
admiration in the new Grump Republic.

Computers

'Sometimes, the only way to get the wi-fi router to work is to jam the laptop right in its face so it can't be ignored. Which rather defeats the object of being wireless. Even then it's less than keen to open a dialogue.'

A Short History of Computers

To put computers in context, I really need to give you a short, byte-sized history of my involvement with them. Don't worry, I'll try and make it as mercifully short as possible.

There was a time when computers filled up whole rooms and were operated by men in white coats. Then came the Sinclair, the ZX81, followed by the ZX Spectrum. My brother had one at the time and the kids who gravitated towards them were the ones who enjoyed double maths, couldn't play football and had their parents' hairstyles. You had to be desperately interested in the binary system to get excited about the early computers. It wasn't like today, where kids retreat to their bedrooms and slay an army of rampaging elves while defending The Mighty Ring of Orcan before tea, and then land a 747 at Singapore Airport after tea.

In the early days, producing a sequence of electronic bleeps in a vague harmonic scale was a bit of a result. By and large, home computers were for neeks, geeks and nerdy freaks.

Then we moved into the realm of the word processing machine and the ubiquitous models produced by Alan Michael Sugar Trading – aka Amstrad. The PCW8256 and PCW8512 were a real improvement to the typewriter. The most brilliant innovation of all was that you could change stuff. Heady days for those of us who had a typewriter at work and kept Tipp-Ex in business.

The first model, as the name suggests, had 256k of memory, a green screen and a dot matrix printer. And then came the model with a dramatically large memory the 512k – yes, half a megabyte! If that wasn't enough we soon got the PCW9512 (which I bought) and that had a daisy wheel printer.

What I still can't work out is why Amstrad didn't go on to conquer the personal computing market, given that they had thousands of happy word processor users who would be more than likely to gravitate to the next Amstrad model to come out. We know that Clive Sinclair got distracted by his laudable (and way ahead of its time) C5, but what stopped Alan from going PC?

PC Gone Mad

Before the advent of Windows, PCs were pretty complicated things; it was Apple Macintoshes that carried the torch of home computing forward. Apple Macs were easy to use, you didn't have to run code, there was a clicky thing called a mouse and you could point it at windows on your screen and the computer got on with stuff. The Mac operating system was intuitive, almost helpful. It was a machine whose creed was "Not for Boffins". Which is why creative people loved it. They didn't have to think about bytes, pixels or RAM, they could just get on and be designery. My first computer was a Mac Classic, which was a tiny all-in-one machine. Looking at the screen was like looking through a letterbox.

Macs improved, then PCs finally got Windows, an easy-to-use Mac-like operating system. The computing market became like the battle of the video format, VHS versus Betamax. Sony's Betamax system was a far superior video format but they didn't licence it widely until it was too late. VHS took hold of the market because the manufacturer, JVC, gave it to everyone.

The same happened with PCs. All kinds of computers could run Windows. Microsoft was smart enough to figure out that it could make all of its money by flogging the software and let Dell and Fujitsu and Hewlett Packard slug it out selling the hardware. The price of hardware soon came down, but you had to pay a premium to buy a Mac with its bespoke operating system. Thus, the PC became the dominant force. Any thoughts Alan Michael may have harboured over ditching the Amstrad video games range and going into computer manufacture were banished forever.

Macs Versus PCs

This partly explains why you get PC versus Mac arguments today. People who have invested big money in their Macs feel they have to justify the investment by droning on about how good they are. PC owners like to taunt them by pointing out that most of the world's software is developed for their computer. It hasn't got as bad as the clan rivalry of the Campbells versus the MacDonalds but it is geekily tribal.

My son is a member of the PC tribe, hating Macs. So for his work experience this year I'm going to get him to come into our office and data cleanse all our old Macs.

Tech-ier Than Thou

Now, you may be thinking after that last bit of spiel (those of you who are still awake) "this Grump geezer likes to come across as a bit of a technophobe, but secretly he's a bit of a nerd". I can only apologise and assure you that any knowledge picked up about the operation and functioning of computers is purely passive nerdism.

Passive nerdism is a bit like passive smoking. You're exposed to computers, you work in the same rooms as them, so you pick up information about them whether you like it or not.

I didn't realise how much passive nerdism had affected me until I was asked to set up a PC for my father-in-law when he was in his mid-seventies. What comes as second nature for someone who's had to work with them for 15 years is utterly bewildering to an older person who's never given them a second thought until badgered by friends to get an email address.

After five years of use it was running slower and slower and I tried to find reasons why. I asked him how often he emptied out his recycle basket and he gave me a blank look. "Empty what…?"

In five years he hadn't. But when I looked in, it was equally odd. Through the five years of use he'd thrown just 25 things away. Judging from the stacks of old newsletters and correspondence in his office, this rule applies to everything in his life.

So, to my father-in-law I am an IT expert. To a real IT expert I am a pain in the butt who asks really stupid questions.

This is the nub of all things technical, whether it be TV remote controls, mobile phones, digital cameras or computers. If you understand something and it didn't take an Open University module to get you to understand it, then it's easy. And anyone who doesn't understand it is stupid.

It's like that famous sketch with Ronnie Corbett, Ronnie Barker and John Cleese from *The Frost Report*, with short Ronnie Corbett representing the working class, medium height Ronnie Barker representing the middle class and tall John Cleese representing the upper class.

For most technologies I'm Ronnie Corbett. When it comes to mobile phones, XBox and gadgets: "I know my place." For a few, such as digital cameras and computers, I'm Ronnie Barker: "I look down on him, but I look up to him." For no technologies am I John Cleese.

Spot the Nerd

You can often spot the John Cleeses* of the techno world in Amazon-style reviews for electronic equipment. This is one that I have blatantly copied from a product review website, changed only slightly, but shortened considerably.

The thing that gets me is that he's not writing to show off at all, he's actually writing to be helpful. But he's not being helpful. It's depressing to think that to understand a product properly you have to burden your grey cells with all that.

This is yet another reason to hate programmes like *The Gadget Show*. They are the pornographers of the techno world, the Paul Raymond Revuebar of electronic gimmickry. If they weren't bigging up all these non-essential toys

---

* Purchased this because Belkin's Router Extender is not Vista Compatible.
It's cheap and can be easily adapted as a Range Extender to fit with any of the 802.11 protocols. First access your own router (see your manual or CD and type in to address bar on Internet Explorer e.g. 192.168.2.1) and write down the IP Address of your router. Also write down subnet mask e.g. 255.255.255.0 and the DHCP Range e.g. 192.168.2.1 to 192.168.2.100. Also a channel number. Go to the Edimax website – choose support-enter 7416APN and download the Set Up Wizard File – it works for Vista and XP. Right-click on the LAN Port and change the TCP/IP properties as on the Edimax instructions to 192.168.2.2.

(Have you got your own helicopter cam yet? We test the three latest models!) the world would be a better place.

*If you've decided to dip in to the text at this point you're probably thinking John Cleese = Basil Fawlty, someone who would be absolutely outraged at the limitations of a computer. You need to read the paragraph above.

The IT Guy

Now I'm not going to suck up to IT guys simply because I think that my own IT guy, Dale, might be reading this book. It's a book, not a manual, he's unlikely to read it. And there's hardly any space to colour in.

IT guys are employed to know a lot about computers, so they have a legitimate excuse for possessing an encyclopaedic knowledge of FTP protocols. But knowledge can be a dangerous thing.

Because they know so much about their chosen profession, dealing with bungling workers who jam DVDs in upside down or delete acres of data and require the backup tapes to be run, or complain that their optical mouse has broken because they're using it on a white surface, can be a little wearing. My sundry grumpiness is nothing compared to the grumpiness of an IT guy.

There is a simmering resentment that they have to deal with organisms on an intellectual par with amoeba and paramecium when they should be doing important work rebuilding the server.

If they had their way, the recruitment criteria for employing new people would start with:

1. A knowledge of Word / Excel / PowerPoint/ PhotoShop
2. The propensity not to crash the system
3. Never getting in touch
4. Nice legs

Computer Helpdesk

It's one of life's rich ironies that the people who man computer helplines tend to be the least suited to a helpline role. The brain that has a thorough knowledge of computer systems isn't the best disposed to talking through simple problems patiently. Putting it another way – you're either a people person or a computer person and the people person with great computer skills or the computer person with great people skills is hard to come by. Certainly, the several I've spoken to checked their customer service manners at the door when they got into work.

Most seem resentful that you rang up in the first place and when your screen doesn't say exactly what their screen is saying they become suspicious and hostile, as though you are somehow concealing information from them, or deliberately pressing the wrong buttons. As if you wanted to somehow prolong this awkward phone call and they were some kind of alternative listening service for when the Samaritans were engaged.

The Celebrated XFi-4B

Of course these are also very easy people to wind up, especially with non-sequiturs thrown into the conversation like confetti. Things like, "You know, I think my RAM is elastic RAM, that's the problem" or "Does using big words make the CPU run slower?"

Having a knowledge of computer terminology is always handy in any situation, whether winding up a computer helpline or looking at the spec of a new computer you are thinking of buying.

Most parameters of a computer are easy to compare: size of hard drive, size of RAM (Random Access Memory), speed of processor, whether single-, dual- or quad-core processor (the more processors the better), number of USB ports, DVD writer, Wi-Fi equipped etc. But then they get to the graphics card. "Features Radical XFi-4B graphics card."

What the hell does that mean?

It could be the top-of-the-range graphics card or it could be entry level. Who knows? The kind of guy who does probably writes reviews like the one we gave earlier.

If you're the kind of person who eagerly awaits the release of a new specification of graphics card then you really should get out more. You can only slaughter so many mystical sword-wielding elves.

Furbished or Refurbished?

Something else that you have to consider these days when upgrading your computer is whether to buy a new one or a refurbished one. Refurbishing is a stupid phrase because it makes it sound like the computer has been used for a time and then recalled for a tune-up, had a few new components slapped in and then stuck in the showroom window – hey presto, refurbished.

Most of them are new units that haven't powered a pixel in their life. Whatever the marketing strategy, they never seem to have the right box for them and they are sent out rattling around with minimum padding by Kamikaze Kouriers inc. I had to send three refurbished PCs back for further refurbishing, till the fourth finally arrived without dents or scrapes garnered in transit.

Not So Quick Plug

Another thing that annoys me about new computers is the places they stick the USB ports. USBs are the friendly little connectors that allow you to plug in printers, keyboards, mice, external hard drives, digital cameras, helicopter cams; the usual must-have accessories of this digital age. Their virtue is that you can plug them straight in and out. So why stick them round the back of the computer in a clump? Brainless. You want lots and you want them out front where you can get at them.

Incidentally, for acronym aficionados, the USB largely replaced the SCSI (Small Computer Serial Interface) connector, which was large and clunky. The USB did to the

SCSI what the HDMI did to the SCART. Feel the love, connector nerds.

Microsoft Omega

One thing that gets superseded on a regular basis with computers is the operating system. Microsoft keep tinkering with theirs to make it less susceptible to the death-is-too-good-for-them scum-suckers who delight in producing computer viruses. But instead of having a neat little sequence of updates (Windows 1, Windows 2, Windows 3 etc.), the corporation have given them distinct identities such as ME Millennium Edition, XP, Vista and now 7. It would have been so much easier if they could have gone from 1 to 7 from the beginning, because as time drags on it's difficult to remember if XP came before or after Vista and so on. You didn't need to have a brain the size of a planet to work that one out.

Software Tinkerers

That's the thing with software guys, they cannot leave be. Now, while I understand the need to constantly upgrade an operating system to make it more robust and resilient to cyber attacks, the same can't be said of word processing software. Microsoft Word is the lingua franca word-processing programme, used the world over.

For me Word 2003 is almost like the King James Bible, it is the *Larousse Gastronomique* of word processing. It does everything I need and many countless things more.

Best of all… I know how to get rid of that irritating "friendly paper clip" office assistant. You know the one I mean? It appears at the top-right corner of the screen waiting to help, its little eyes and raised eyebrows indicating that it is eager to help, but only irritating the hell out of you.

Click on it and a little dialogue box comes up that reads, "What would you like me to do…?" As you type in "kill yourself", it studiously goes and finds itself a pencil and a piece of paper and begins to write a note on three lines. At the end it looks at you with a slightly quizzical look. Interestingly the No.1 piece of advice it goes off and finds when you type in "kill yourself" is how to turn off the Assistant.

Word 2003 doesn't need updating but that doesn't stop Microsoft from tinkering around with it and making it "better" by installing new features, and changing some of the old. Oh no, that's not the way to make money. Thus, now I have Word 2010 in the office and Word 2003 at home and my PC at home is even more disgusted than I am with the changes and says it's NOT going to engage with my work documents because it refuses to recognise the file extension. So I've got a Mexican standoff between my two computers while work is slipping through my fingers.

Laptop Batteries

I tell you what, if technology companies devoted half the time they spend reconfiguring software on making laptop batteries last longer, that would be a real leap forward. They seem to be able to do everything with a laptop except this. They can make the screens wider and thinner. They can make the bodies thinner and lighter. They can give them desktop PC-size hard drives, Wi-Fi connectivity, DVD drives, an XFi-4B graphics card (you know, the really good one). With the modern laptop the world is at your fingertips, for about 40 minutes and then the battery warning light flashes up, like the man from the costume shop who used to appear at the end of the *Mr Benn* adventures to tell him that time was up.

This has forced many laptop owners into outright energy theft. There is a breed of laptop owner that seeks out plug sockets wherever they can. You see them umbilically attached in public areas of airports, stations and on ferries. Underground or overground, they go wombling around for some free kilowatts. Charge 'em, that's what I say (that's money, not electricity).

The Andy Warhol Laptop Battery

Battery life is one of those take-with-a-pinch-of-salt figures you read in any laptop's sales blurb. You can normally divide it in two. It's like the 0-60 acceleration figure for a road car, which they get by using a jockey-sized driver who crash-changes the gearbox in a driving display you would never ever emulate yourself... unless it was a hire car.

The calculation of battery life is presumably done at optimum temperature with the laptop powering a minimalist screensaver. Not with some teenager repelling wave after wave of alien droids in a hardcore, dual-core max-ing it out, beat'em up computer game.

Andy Warhol said that we would all be famous for 15 minutes. He meant that's how long our laptop batteries would stay charged.

Lies, Damned Lies, and Broadband Speeds

It's the same with a lot of computer-related technology and in particular broadband speeds. The phrase "Up to 20 megabytes a second" from your Internet service providers really means, "It'll never get up to 20 megabytes a second." It might get close when you log on at 3am on Monday, but most of the time it'll hover around 4 megabytes a second, then drop out completely when you want to book some once-in-a-lifetime concert tickets the moment the online box office opens.

The other great underachiever of the computer peripheral world is the Wi-Fi router. This is the device that attaches to your modem and pretends to send signals round the house to Wi-Fi enabled devices.

The Wi-Fi router is the operatic diva of the computer world. It performs when it wants to perform, there is no second-guessing what it will do next. Sometimes it behaves beautifully and gives you range to the bottom of the garden and in every room of the house. Sometimes it won't perform even up close. It is an infuriating object that spreads its miserable vicissitudes to other members of the household.

Drag-A-Chair Bear

Since buying herself a bright pink laptop, the Wi-Fee has become incredibly interested in the Wi-Fi. When she's not outside collecting leaves off the drive or chasing up possibly the worst builder in the world (see *The Grumpy Gardener's Handbook* for the full exposition) she trails round the house clutching her laptop like Drag-a-chair Bear. Drag-a-chair was a baby bear character from *Wizzer and Chips* comic who would always drag a small chair around the bear household. My wife does the same with her treasured Sony Vaio held out front, in the unfurled position.

Most of the time she'll be walking about trying to get connectivity and moaning about the state of her bars. "I've got five bars but nothing's happening" is something she likes to say a lot.

"Oh," I'll reply with a simulated concern in my voice, not knowing what this really means and, to be honest, not really caring. However, I know that failure to acknowledge her lack of megabytes-per-second without sufficient gravity doesn't go down very well. I know Drag-a-chair will find connectivity sooner or later and the last resort is to place her laptop right next to the diva-like router, so it has no option but to supply her.

An Internet What Provider...?

What is it with Internet Service Providers (ISPs)? If we are to believe the government about the future being digital and how everyone should have access to broadband, then maybe it would be good to have professionals providing our Internet services.

When I go to turn on a light I expect the electricity to be there. The electricity providers don't occasionally turn the electricity off to do essential maintenance – without telling me. Neither do they supply just a fraction of the electricity I need because 'too many people are using electricity at the same time'. It's a service and they provide it constantly.

The same goes with water and gas, it's not disconnected on a whim only to return mysteriously an hour later. So why is it so difficult for ISPs to maintain a constant supply of Internet? It goes down without warning and then suddenly reappears again. If a TV programme gets interrupted for just a few seconds then there's an apology and an explanation. For the ISPs, nothing.

And the disruption can be enormous. At first you think it's your browser, so you switch from Firefox to Chrome. Still nothing. Then you think it might be your computer, which you close down and restart. Then you start giving your modem a hard time, followed by a fiddle with the router. If all this fails you go round checking that all the leads and connections are plugged in properly, after which the only conclusion is that your ISP has cut the service.

In the Grump Republic ISPs would have to refund you an entire month's charges if they dropped out for five minutes or more. That would certainly concentrate their attention on maintaining the system properly and having a back-up system that was better than two Sinclair Spectrums wired together.

How Clean Is Your...Computer?

It wouldn't be an exhilarating half hour on television but it might be quite useful. *How Clean Is Your House?* introduced us to Kim and Aggie, two redoubtable cleaning ladies who tackled the most stubborn of stains. In particular, they tackled the houses these useless stains lived in. They set about restoring cleanliness and order to rooms that had gone way beyond "a right old state".

Somebody should do the same for technology in the home.

Get a couple of personable nerds, two excellent broadcasters with computer skills – let's call them John and Jason – and get them to run a technology audit on households.

First and foremost on their plan of action would be to have a look at the family's computers to check they were running efficiently, not stuffed up with memory-clogging programmes they don't use, or harbouring nasty viruses. They could look at the positioning of the truculent Wi-Fi router and advise on where to put it in the house to get the best coverage.

They could look at phone systems, TV and entertainment centres and maybe suggest a few innovations that the family hasn't thought about – such as easy-to-install motion-triggered light switches to save energy.

It wouldn't necessarily have the dramatic peeping-through-fingers-in-horror of the grisly kitchen scenes from *How Clean Is Your House?*, but there would be a small band of nerds around the country wailing in fright as they discover that somebody has installed an XFi-4B graphics card without sufficient RAM.

Small Is Beautiful

One thing we can be grateful to the laptop for is driving down the size of computer components. This search for ever-smaller, neater laptops has slimmed down the desktop PC enormously. What was once a box the size of a small carry-on suitcase (that's carry onto an aircraft not *Carry On PC World*) has now been reduced to the size of a DVD box set. Whereas my last desktop PC had to be installed using a forklift truck, the current "space-saving" upgraded version could probably have been lugged into place by a tech-friendly squirrel. Well, you can train them to do complex things to get at nuts, plugging in a few cables with their dextrous little paws shouldn't be too hard.

What amazes me is why some computer manufacturers still produce huge, unnecessarily large housings for their desktop PCs. It's a fact that Britain has the smallest amount of room space per head of population in Europe. When it comes to the G20 countries we're only saved from bottom place by Japan and there's 120 million of them. So, Acer, HP, Fujitsu: make them smaller, you know you can.

Protection Racket

Something that is far more annoying than stupidly large computers is the protection software racket. These companies are supposed to make you feel snug and warm about your computer, safe from harmful viruses and the stoats and weasels* of the Wild Wood that is cyberspace.

They come on all concerned and caring with their 30 days of free protection. Then when you've decided you don't want to continue after the free trial, they turn ugly. It's Glenn

---

* *While we're at it, what did Kenneth Graham have against stoats and weasels?* Wind in the Willows *gave me the long-lasting impression that they were nasty, evil creatures whereas in reality they're tiny cute creatures, much under threat from man. Okay, they steal a bird's egg here or there, that's hardly a crime. If Ken wanted to have a go at badgers then no problem, they are big and ugly and can look after themselves, but Ken, leave it out with the stoats.*

Close in *Fatal Attraction* all over again. They send you emails telling you that your existing firewall is shoddy; they run scans and tell you about threats they've detected on your computer (probably a cookie from a harmless supermarket website that displays their advert). They are like The Sopranos of the Internet world – they're pretending to offer protection while really they're extorting money off you based on your fear of what might happen if you don't get protected. When you try and uninstall the programme from your computer, Big Sal Bonpensiero comes round and says, "Oh, I found your dog, here he is."

These companies need to know it's over. Deal with it.

Blue Screen of Death

The most awful thing to happen when you own a computer is the blue screen of death. When your computer expires it is undoubtedly a painful and traumatic experience, so it's best to get it over with when you're young. In many ways it's like having a pet. When a pet dies you learn to cope with the grief and this is a useful life lesson.

When your computer dies it teaches you a lot more lessons, in particular it teaches you to back up your blinking hard drive! While a failed motherboard, faulty RAM or processor can be replaced, a cooked hard drive turns all those binary switches into mush. I know of friends who have lost four or five years' worth of digital images because their hard drive decided it wanted to make a Buddhist transition and become a toaster or a WWII incendiary.

There's no excuse either – external hard drives cost so little per gigabyte. The cost is coming down all the time.

You can get a terabyte of storage – that's 1,000 gigabytes – for under £60. Amazing.

The only problem comes when you take on board the fact that no hard drive is forever – and that if you want a belt-and-braces storage solution for your treasured pictures, home movies, letters etc., you're going to have to write them onto a DVD. And then you've got to hope that DVDs last, unlike floppy disks and Zip disks.

The Internet

'How wantonly indulgent do you have to be
to congratulate your own daughter on her GCSE
results on Facebook? When you still live in the same
house, that kind of thing can be expressed verbally.
This doesn't appear to be enough now that
we have social networking.'

A foray into the grumpy world of the computer wouldn't be complete without a look at the worldwide web. There are many marvellous innovations that the Internet has brought us. I'm not going to focus on any of them.

What I am going to look at is the unmentionable rubbish it has heaped on our lives. Luckily for you I'm not Leo Tolstoy (who in real life was a bit of a Russian grumpy git). A thousand pages on the evils of the Internet would have been just warming up for Leopold. I'll try and keep to under the thousand.

Middle-Aged Men on Facebook

I can see why children and teenagers like it, I can see why young adults who are still "out there" like it, I can see why sociable women of all ages like it. I cannot understand why middle-aged men should be on it. Those married men who do have Facebook pages are either creepily flirtatious or have mild ADD, but usually both.

Ivor Grump liked this.

Women are gregarious creatures who are naturally sociable. They form themselves into groups such as book clubs, or babysitting circles, or like-minded mums, so for them it's a perfect venue for yet more social interaction. Men don't trade tittle-tattle very easily, so you have to suspect their motives for going on there.

The only reason I'm able to comment on Facebook is that

my wife has allowed me to delve into her page and apart from the sad, middle-aged men that occasionally float by on the tide, there are the hopeless self-publicists.

Ivor Grump commented on Mrs Grump's status.

Pass The Sick Bucket!

How wantonly indulgent do you have to be to congratulate your own daughter on her GCSE results on Facebook? When you still live in the same house that kind of thing can be expressed verbally. This doesn't appear to be enough now that we have social networking. "Well done on your fabulous GCSE results Mirabella, I'm so proud of you."

Once this is posted, there is a strange etiquette that unfolds where Mirabella's mother's friends are obliged to join in and say something suitably upbeat, while some of them – including my wife – will be thinking "stupid cow".

Ivor Grump has posted something on Mrs Grump's wall.

I also came across the kind of posts that were so nauseating that they were an art form rivalling anything Damien Hirst could concoct. They were posted by a wife thanking her husband for a wonderful night out with their two beautiful children at a concert followed by a lovely family dinner for four at a top London restaurant. She just wanted to say (and for all her friends to know) that she'd had an absolutely fantastic time and she loved him so, so very much. It was as cringeworthy as anything Ricky Gervais could have dreamt up.

That wasn't all. In reply, the husband posted back that he, too, thought it was an overwhelmingly fantastic occasion and that he was the luckiest man alive and so lucky to have her as a wife.

So saccharin was the moment, that you began to wonder if it was hiding a bitter truth and the knuckle-bitingly gruesome Facebook commentary was an exercise in wallpapering over the cracks – giving it one last go for the sake of their ugly children. Because if you take my first premise as correct – that it is only creepily flirtatious middle-aged men who devote time to their Facebook pages – then it's highly likely he's been trying to play away.

* Ivor Grump wanted to create a Bleargh! button.
* Mrs Grump liked this.

Poke Her Mom

Then of course there is all this business of giving someone a poke. You can give someone a poke and they can give you a poke back. This has all the bucolic charm of wearing a smock, sitting on a dry stone wall, and getting your three-tined implement ready to give someone a gurt big poke. My daughter regularly pokes my wife. My wife pokes her back. I never give my wife a poke.

If this was still the 1960s the French could probably make a 90-minute enigmatic *film noir* on this basic premise.

Pop-ups

It's worth investing in some Internet security to get rid of pop-ups alone. Pop-up adverts are annoying for all sorts of reasons, but mainly because they get in your way and you have to do something to get rid of them, you can't just ignore them like you can the rest of the ads. They are the door-to-door salesmen of the Internet world. Advertisers pay a premium for them and it's hard to know why because they are so antagonistic. I can't think of one pop-up advert that I looked at and thought "hmm, that's interesting" and then clicked through.

Deliberately, that is.

There were some online casino adverts for a while that had a false "Close" button. You pressed it hoping to get rid of the infernal pop-up and instead it opened another window, or clicked through to the main casino site, trying to suck you in further.

There are many ways that people can get hooked on gambling, but not being able to get rid of an on-screen pop-up is a poor reason.

Hooked On Porn

A similar kind of device can hook you into porn sites. While being taken to gambling sites is a pain in the backside, it's irritating and annoying more than anything else. When you get sucked into porn sites it induces sheer panic. You immediately think that the wife is going to walk in on you, and immediately deduce that this is what you're up to for three hours every night... and why you wanted to increase your broadband speed. Or your daughter is going to come and ask you for some paper for her homework and the bond between father and daughter is going to be broken forever. The "I was just doing some research" excuse wouldn't work in our household.

So when over-tanned limbs and gravity-defying breasts appear for no reason on screen it's a frantic scramble to get them off. You click back, nothing happens; you click back again, nothing happens. You try to close it, it doesn't. You click somewhere else, it's worse. Ooooh, much worse. "How can they do that...?" you wonder tilting your head for a second, then realise what you're doing. "No, no, get it away!" At which point you yank the power cable out of the back of the computer as a sure fire way to end it all and save the marriage and relationship with your daughter.

This is no exaggeration. The mortal fear that overcomes me when I accidentally stray onto a porn site would be highly comical if covered by a webcam. Not one that I hooked up, mind you, because you'd probably get three hours coverage of the edge of my keyboard.

Calm Down Dear, it's Just a Commercial

Porn is very big on the Internet now because it doesn't involve shuffling into the newsagents and buying a top-shelf item. Something similar that has enjoyed a massive boom is car insurance via the web.

To establish themselves in the market and make their presence known, the Internet companies had to spend a fortune on advertising. Television is obviously an effective way of getting the message across. Thus we got the ever-decreasing Michael Winner sashaying onto screen with his famous, "Calm down dear, it's just a commercial" line. The adverts were intentionally clunky, but they certainly caught your attention.

In fact, their huge success led to other insurance companies or price comparison websites devising similarly dreadful adverts you couldn't eradicate from your mind. How else could you explain the Confused.com adverts?

These have gradually become better and better as we have got more sophisticated in our choices. We know to buy our insurance on the web these days, the advertising is all about getting us to switch brands. So we get the Churchill ads, the Go Compare ads, the fabulous More Than (Freeman) ads and the wonderful Compare the Meerkat ads. The meerkat ads have been so successful that they have spawned a best-selling book and more people go to Compare the meerkat.com than go to Compare the market.com. Getting people to type in that particularly long URL was always going to be a toughie but they did it.

Comparisons Are Odious

They may suck people in with clever advertising, but insurance comparison websites can be frustrating and time-wasting things. For a start they never compare the whole market because some of the key players in the insurance business opt out. Thus you may get the cheapest of the brands that are included but competitive companies like Direct Line aren't in there.

Whenever I've used them for a price comparison I've spent half an hour putting in all kinds of details – engine size, mileage, hat size, the full nine yards. After giving more information to them than is included on my CV it spits out the result that there was no suitable insurance for my Ford Mondeo. We're not talking about a Lamborghini Murciélago here, this is one of the most common cars sold in the UK! I think the thing that spooks them out is that I want 15 days of cover in Europe every year and this must be too bizarre a request for the computer to handle. All they want is the core, easy, low-hanging fruit of the middle market, nothing too fancy, nothing that smacks of being a service to consumers.

I would never ever go back to using them, for me it's an exercise in wasting time. The only time I have ever got a computation from them (I caved in on the 15 days abroad), another insurance company beat them by about £50.

Grumpipedia

Sometimes the accuracy of Wikipedia isn't exactly what you'd expect from such a universal reference tool. I thought I might create my own profile using the Wikipedia tolerances for accuracy.

Ivor Grump: Author of the Grumpy Guide Book series. Ivor Grump lives on the Isle of Wight. He is married with seven children. His wife, often referenced in the Grumpy Notebook series, has various pet names including 'The Apostrophe Nazi' and 'Branch Lady' after an OCD for shaking branches. There are six books in the Grumpy series, four by Ivor and one by his brother Cedric, who was run over by a train in an unfortunate level crossing incident in 2007.

Grumpy Handbooks: *One Grump or Two* by Cecil Grump; *Grumpy Driver's Handbook*, *Grumpy Gopher's Handbook*, *Grumpy Gardener's Handbook*, *The Grumpy Git's Guide to Technology*, all by Ivor Grump.

Career: Ivor has made a career out of being grumpy. He blames the sport of golf, the misery of which he chronicled in Grumpy Cricketer's Notebook.

Interests: He is keen on promoting civil liberties and furthering the uptake of digital technology.

eBay

I love eBay and have been buying stuff through their website across two millennia. All right, since 1999. (Cue the music for the Hovis advert.) Of course it was better in the old days...

No, it really was. The system might not have been as user friendly as it is today, giving you a second-by-second countdown to the moment you are going to be outbid, but back in 1999 the postal charges didn't make your heart sink. You could buy an inexpensive item and the postage didn't add that much on. Not any more. P&P makes a big difference. Every time I buy a stamp today I think, "this is going into the big black hole that is the postal pensions fund". But then again every time I go and park my car in the city centre and look at the charges per hour I go scurrying back to my computer.

For shoppa-phobes like myself, online shopping is the greatest thing. A few clicks of the computer and there it is, bought. Apart from saving a lot of time and energy it brings me into contact with so many nationalities of delivery driver.

The best deliveries of all are those that arrive at 7am on

a Saturday morning. Mrs Grump is a big fan of those.

eBay is not perfect and there are a few things that I'd change. That opening gambit after you have placed the initial bid in an auction: "You're the first bidder – hope you win" seems a bit vacuous to me. Do they really hope I win or are they just saying that? You know, I think they're just saying that and I'm not the favourite son I thought I was for the first five years on eBay.

'No.1 E.Bayer A*!'

There are elements of the feedback system that could be improved that's for certain. People say the stupidest things. "No.1 Ebayer!" or "A+++ transaction, will use again!" Yawn. I try and inject a bit of humour into mine yet without deflecting from the serious message of appreciation. For products sent from China I never miss the opportunity for a little bit of agitprop, a message to the glorious workers and entrepreneurs such as: "May you thrive with the spirit of Mao in your hearts."

You might be surprised to learn that for such a grumpy b*****d I very rarely give negative feedback. The feedback system has left people paranoid about getting anything less than a 99 per cent satisfaction rating, so eBay listings are unique amongst most sales blurbs in that the sellers actively point to all the faults on an item. They photograph the scrapes and scuffs in loving detail so that you are forewarned.

Sometimes they forget to promote the item they're selling in the rush to acquaint you with all the bad bits.

When you read some of the negative feedback it's usually left by stupid people who didn't know what they were buying. The key to this is to look at their eBay rating. I wouldn't mind betting that 80 per cent of the negative feedback is left by people with a rating of under 20. Both eBay and IQ.

When you see negative feedback from somebody with a very high rating then you sit up and take notice.

Bote Four Sail

The other great insight eBay gives you into our culture is the failure of our education system. There is an excuse for bad spelling on message boards and online chatrooms because you are just bashing off an instant message with very little thought. That, after all, is one of the main prerequisites for being in an online chatroom – having very little thought.

When you're constructing an advert to sell something then it demands a little more care. It would be good if your spelling was above the level of Winnie the Pooh and Piglet in *The House at Pooh Corner*, for example.

eBay could help by including a spellchecker in their advertising engine. They already have one in their product search. I'm a big fan of moody French photographer Jean-Francois Jonvelle. Type that into the eBay search bar and you end up looking at 50 varieties of Jonelle king-size sheets with matching pillow case sets.

In the interests of further education I think eBay should ban people who produce adverts with more than five spelling errors. We all had the opportunity of a state education when we were young. It's not like the old days when most children were sent down the pits at the age of 10. Even if they lived in Dorset.

My wife – the apostrophe Nazi – would probably have

them serving some kind of custodial sentence for that; although she seems to conserve most of her ire these days for badly worded letters from the school. I'm not sure how easily the European Court of Human Rights would take to the concept of punctuation prisons or grammar prisons, but I suspect I would be heading there in a matter of months.

People Who Bought This...

One of the interesting things about buying stuff on Amazon is a kind of consumer voyeurism. Having bought a CD of say, *The Best of Buffalo Springfield*, you can see what: 'Customers who bought this CD also bought…'

I ought to point out right here and now that Buffalo Springfield were way before my time and I was in a bit of a retro Sixties mood. The group included Stephen Stills and Neil Young and so the CDs that follow in the Amazon 'Customers who bought' panel are typically by Crosby, Stills, Nash and Young, Joni Mitchell, Stephen Stills solo albums and Neil Young solo albums etc. All very predictable.

What is really interesting is when you buy more obscure records. With the bigger artistes, where the weight of consumer numbers flattens out anything quirky, you are unlikely to get: 'Customers who bought a Michael Bublé album also bought *Never Mind the Bollocks, Here's the Sex Pistols*. As far as I know Michael Bublé has never covered *Anarchy in the UK* or any other of the Pistols' back catalogue, demonstrating yet again that the Ukelele Orchestra of Great Britain are way ahead of the Bublé.

But if you buy something a bit more niche, like an album by Southend's greatest ever troubadors, the Kursaal

Flyers, you don't know where you might end up; Country, Jazz, Rockabilly, 1970s retro, Pub Rock Heroes... it's a rollercoaster. This is the serendipitous joy of Amazon. Is it any surprise that HMV went down the tubes so rapidly when you can actually browse titles, read track info, and listen to snippets of music in the comfort of your own pyjamas on a Saturday morning? Obviously whilst browsing in HMV you don't have to endure the kind of toadying sycophantic reviews you get on Amazon, but when the local council has upped the parking charges to £2.80 an hour (Hammersmith), it's a much smaller price to pay.

Frequently Bought versus iTunes Recommends

Having looked again at Amazon, there are more helpful purchasing suggestions along with the 'Customers who bought this' panel. There is the 'Frequently bought together' panel which gives you a little purchasing nudge. There is also the 'Customers who shopped for this, also shopped for...' panel which gives an insight into what other people are browsing for, not just ordering.

I'm quite happy to be sold stuff in this way. It's a commercial site, I'm in a buying mood and I've certainly gone on and bought CDs I never knew existed and discovered music I really like thanks to their suggestions. What I can't stand is iTunes Recommends.

If you go into a shop you expect to be sold things. When you go to your record player you don't expect it to start poking you and pointing you in the direction of other music.

I've never put on a CD of the Eagles and found my CD player telling me I ought to buy some of Bernie Leadon's other work. That's what I get with the genius of iTunes. (Incidentally iTunes have their music guide 'Ping' and Microsoft have their search engine 'Bing', something's got to give there.)

Ivor Grump vs Mullet-Headed Radio 1

Driving with teenagers in the car I'm forced to listen to Radio 1 from time to time. No matter how much I ask, they never provide me with ear defenders and so some of the rubbish goes in and actually sticks. One of the unfathomably stupid developments is to have DJ Battles. One DJ plays a track, another DJ plays a track and they argue the case for each of their tracks. Yawn. Then you can tweet or text in to say which you liked best, or if they can't be arsed, they'll decide between themselves which was the No.1. Hardly a battle is it? I don't recall battles between the Greeks and the Carthaginians being settled by Pompeii going, "all right Hannibal, you've set up your troops in a much more advantageous position with my left flank exposed, go on then, I'll give you this one."

It's about as stupid as two announcers on Radio 3 (they can't possibly have DJs on Radio 3) going head to head with a composers' battle. Handel versus Wagner – yeah, bring it on George. Sez who? Gonna make me, Richard?

Or maybe they should have folk battles. You could get Radio 2's Mike Harding slamming Rambling Syd Rumpo's classic 'One, Two Me Deario' onto the turntable against the Boggle Hole Chorale's 'It's Harvesting Time'.

Amazon-Style Ratings

Letting the public loose to write their own opinions about products on sites like Amazon is good, but like all things, a bit of censorship never hurt anyone. I'm always suspicious of the glowing report and equally suspicious of the damning rebuke. You need to steer a course somewhere between the two.

The five-star review posted just weeks after a product has been launched is always to be viewed with a bit of scepticism – what if this gizmo has tremendous features but breaks down after a month. Not so five-star then, is it…? I always suspect that someone from the manufacturer goes on and waxes lyrical about their precious new item. The key things to look for are:

Are there any negative aspects to it. All products have limitations. This book, though consistently marvellous and hysterical from start to finish, has no colour pictures.

What items has this person reviewed before? If it's nothing else, then those alarm bells should be ringing.

There are also some brilliant mickey-take Amazon reviews out there aimed squarely at the po-faced and opinionated reviewer who likes the sound of his own prejudice (no, that's not me). You can buy Bic biros on Amazon, which is one of the things you really don't need to review. So, in steps the comedy reviewer who lambasts them for not having enough fonts available on the biro. The same treatment is given to a lot of run-of-the-mill stationery equipment, with some paper considered too white and some reviewers disgusted that their white paper wasn't white enough.

I'm Your Biggest Sycophant

Some of the worst abuses of the review system crop up in the music section. To keep it short: there are so many bottom lickers out there. When you're undecided about taking the plunge on buying a CD from an artist you don't know very well (yes, very old school, the whole CD, not three MP3 downloads. Ivor Grump keepin' music alive, man) it's nice to get a bit of guidance. After the inestimable Radcliffe and Maconie disappeared off Radio 2 in the evenings, to be replaced by the sneery blonde, I've reverted back to listening to more CDs.

The trouble is, you go on Amazon, and most of the reviews are five star. Even albums you know are a load of old bananas get five stars. The only album I can guarantee won't have five stars without actually checking is Elton John's *Victim of Love*, which I hurled out of the window crossing the Severn Bridge one time. It was the tape version, not the vinyl, I hasten to add. That really was the biggest load of old toot – Elton goes Giorgio Moroder – and ended a beautiful relationship with the recording artist, never to be renewed.

With everything rated the same on Amazon it's difficult to know where to start with an artist who's had 20 or 30 years making records. I really want to listen to more Leonard Cohen, but I might as well flip a coin than go by the Amazon reviews. (As a small grumpy aside, Tony Palmer's fabulous film of Cohen on the road in the early 1970s shows: a) what a brilliant talent he had, and, more interestingly, b) how sensationally grumpy he got with his audiences. This is an artist who hated people clapping when they recognised his songs at the beginning and stopped to tell his audience off. I want to buy his records for that alone!)

Cruising for a Bruising

Travel Advisor reviews are a lot more useful than Amazon ones. I don't think I'd book anywhere now without checking the place out on their website first. Again, you have to use a bit of judgement when reading some of the reviews, especially when there are not that many, but it's always going to be more accurate than the brochure.

There is a similar kind of website that accumulates customer reviews for the cruising market – and by cruising I mean cruise ships, not the Norfolk Broads or any other cruising activity. We went on one last year, though I can't name the company for legal reasons.

As we approached the ship, my wife pointed to the portholes very close to the waterline. "We'll be much higher than that" I reassured her, "those'll be the crew cabins." In fact, she was probably pointing directly at our cabin. I'm not saying they were old and small but it was very reminiscent of an early 1980s caravan holiday – that's a touring caravan, not a static. Parts of the ship were 1980s, parts of it were 1990s and a few lounges had been updated in the last decade to give a hotchpotch of styles.

There was a throbbing vibration that ran through the ship, which didn't bother me at all, but irritated some people. On a cruise ship scale we were particularly small and decidedly old. When we arrived in Venice and got parked next to three other massive palaces of the seas its passengers were staring down at us from five decks higher.

The entertainment director on the ship was German and brought with him all the easy humour that comes so naturally to Germans. For a cruise, the food was pretty average, and the entertainment was sub-Butlin's (who I used to work for in the 1980s and still have a great affection for). On the plus side, the day trips that were organised from each port were really good, not a rip-off like they are with some cruise companies. And because we were small we could get into a lot of the ports the other cruise ships couldn't, so the itinerary was great.

When we got back, I put all these thoughts down in a review on the cruising website. Some good points, some bad and some humorously bad. Within an hour, ALL the negative points had been answered by "other customers". In a string of posts below my review; the food, the cabins, the awful German director and the entertainment had been defended to the hilt. I thought "aye aye – that looks a bit suspicious", one person defending a ship they've had a good time on is fair enough – but five, straight away…?

I'm not going to spell it out.

From Ports to Portals

Portal sites are pretty irritating, too. They are the neutered male cats of the Internet world, they don't provide any kind of service, they just get in the way. Basically, they're cyber squatters sitting on a good website name hoping that one day someone will come along and offer them a bundle of cash for it. In the meantime, they'll pretend they're of some use by collecting together a load of links vaguely connected to their subject.

You – the surfer – are Googling around looking for information on, say, mangelwurzels. You see a website named mangelwurzels.co.uk. "Wow", you think, you've hit the nail right on the head here. They'll have everything you need to know about mangelwurzels and so you click on it. The single drab page that loads is a list of vaguely related websites on a variety of things: how to grow root vegetables, how to repair old mangles, the Wurzels, Thomas Hardy and then a link to Everest Double Glazing.

News, What News?

Not quite as useless but still pretty irritating is the BBC website. For an organisation famed for its news reporting, the hard news stories fare very badly compared to the features they run online. You'd think that someone in the newsroom might twig something was wrong when feature items like, "Can Cats Count?" is No. 2 in their Top Ten stories table, ahead of almost all the political and economic reporting of the day.

Quite regularly it's only the shocking news – the murders, the battles, the earthquakes – that make it ahead of the most mundane of features about rude Germans or how big bottoms have been linked to longevity.

The other day – and I kid you not – the top story was...Chris Evans being half an hour late for his radio programme. At the time there were major new stories in Northern Ireland, about the NHS, Japan and Iceland, but no, the only thing they could really make readable was a story about how a disc jockey got his starting time wrong. (It was a Saturday, not his familiar weekday programme.)

This was followed a close second by a story about a pub landlord who thought he had an elephant buried in his car park. These are clearly the stories people want to read and they don't come to the website for more of the same preachy, right-on, politically correct news items that are broadcast on radio and television.

As a vehicle for BBC programme output it's fine. Who could not love the BBC iPlayer and the opportunity to listen to TV and radio programmes that you missed? (Well done the BBC, worth the licence fee alone etc.) But when they generate items themselves they mess it up.

Readers of *Grumpy Gardener*, please excuse me trotting this one out again, but the person in charge of the icons on the weather page has got a pretty odd sense of humour. You look to see what the weather will be like two days ahead and you have the sunny icon; look on the site again at lunchtime and it has the cloudy icon; by mid-afternoon it has the drizzle icon and by five o'clock it will have the storm and pestilence icon. The next day – just one day away now – and it has the sunny icon again. When it comes to the day itself there will be fog. I think perhaps the icons are randomly generated (using Guinevere).

Cookies or Cling-ons?

There is an Internet device called a "cookie" which sits on your computer waiting for its opportunity to shine. It's a clever little devil that works hand in hand with your Internet browser to remember stuff about past websites you visited. Calling it a cookie makes it sound nice and wholesome, something you might want on your computer. Because if you called it a Cling-on or a Limpet or an Info-Leech it might not seem quite so innocuous. Cookies are the things responsible for delivering dedicated adverts to some of the websites you browse. For example, I bought a pair of steel-capped wellingtons from the Screwfix catalogue and when next I went on to the Planet-F1 website, in the side column there was an advert for Screwfix.

Funny, I thought, I hadn't noticed that on the website before. Bit of a coincidence that. Then I bought the wife some lingerie for her birthday from the Marks and Spencer website. The next thing I knew every website I went on had an advert for M&S lingerie at the side. Not for M&S Blue Harbour loafers or formal suits or ready meals, no, exactly the kind of lingerie I'd been surveying for the wife. Then the penny dropped…

Now, because the wife uses my computer as well as her Drag-a-chair Bear laptop I had to go onto the Marks and Spencer website and create a smokescreen. So I browsed through pages and pages of mildly offensive slippers, sometimes pulling them up to look at their fluffy top view in great detail to confirm my interest. My cookie bought it. Next time I went on Hotmail, up came a satisfying sidebar, an array of slippers that the late lamented Nora Batty couldn't have turned down.

Match.com

Knowing what I know, I can't help but feel undermined. After she's been on the computer looking at her emails I get the sidebar adverts for Match.com. What's going on there? How can I NOT be the perfect match when I regularly replace my smelly old Wellingtons…?

Twitter

How much do I hate twitter and tweeting? There's another word beginning with "tw" that fully describes the majority of people who do it.

There was a fabulous book someone published a while back called *Boring Postcards*, showcasing some of the most pointless postcards every produced. These were postcards of telecommunication masts from the 1960s, blocks of flats that the local council were proud of or bland industrial estates. It was a feast of mesmerisingly dull images that made you wonder why anyone ever bothered. Tweets are like the electronic equivalent.

I concede that someone with the eloquence and verbal dexterity of Stephen Fry could be entertaining in 140 characters and it might be fun to hear what they're up to from time to time. Everyone else…?

Tweets are only funny in that they constantly get Premiership footballers into trouble because nobody censors what they say before they go out. The first time you hear about it is when the footballer in question has to delete his tweet and apologise for any offence caused. The referees association must have to follow all of them. Poor loves, they have a hard enough time as it is.

The Tweet Smell of Excess

Safe to say that tweeting would be banned in the Grump Republic. Tweeting, like many things in the modern digital world, takes up time when we could be thinking.

These days, it seems, nature abhors a vacuum of information or digital interaction. If we go on a journey we need to access emails and phonecalls along the way, we need video games or movies on our phones to stop us being bored, and we need our own music from MP3 players to drown out the soundtrack of the world around us. And some of us, it turns out, need to tweet that we have just got into the car and there's more traffic than we expected.

Take the children out to a restaurant for the evening and they're all fidgeting to get at their phones. The second we arrive home they all dive for their bedrooms to get online and see what they've missed on Facebook, or recharge their phone which has run down in the restaurant.

In my book, a good slice of boredom and isolation never hurt anyone.

It's a Crutch

How did Radio DJs get by before texting and tweets? Should you have the misfortune to listen to Radio 1 – no, let me put that another way – should you endure the calamity of being exposed to Radio 1 for any length of time, you realise that they have become dependent on tweets and texts. They are the ephemeral crutch on which the shows depend. They play the latest single by the Arctic Monkeys and you can text in your thoughts: Jo studying for exams in Cardiff loved it; Nathan eating pizza in Hull thought it wasn't as good as the last one; Simon travelling to Glasgow on the M8 says it's the best yet.

Who the Hell Cares?

They only use texts to show that they have more than five listeners and that these listeners are based right around the country and not all in London. If they get texts or emails from people listening on the Internet around the world they love it even more. They are like some desperate, fat, unpopular kid at school shouting out "Look, I have got friends! I really have got friends!"

Using texts means all they have to do is ask questions and get the listeners to provide the show rather than coming up with some original content themselves.

Printers

'Our photocopier is irritatingly eager. When you send something to print, it adopts the persona of a Labrador dog that has just seen you pick up a tennis ball. It activates the receiving trays and they all move up and down to show you how good they are at moving up and down.'

Everyone needs a few peripherals and a printer is a must-have peripheral. In the good old days of the Amstrad PCW, the bottom-of-the-range model came with a dot matrix printer that was the Cro-Magnon man of the species; everything would be better evolved and more sophisticated from that point on. Print something on that and it made you look like an Open University Maths lecturer.

A step up from the lamentable dot matrix was the daisywheel printer, which had all the letters on thin plastic spines around the edge of a circle, making them look like the petals of a daisy – or, if you want to be very nit-picky, an aster, which is bigger than a daisy. The petals used to break off and never because "she loves me".

From there we moved to inkjet and laser printers, more refined inkjet printers and then to inkjet printer/scanners with phenomenal capabilities. What's more, the price of printers fell through the floor.

But for every yin, there is a yang. The low cost of the hardware was accompanied by a staggering hike in the cost of "consumables". Once equipped with your all-singing, all-scanning printer, purchased for a song, you had to pay an arm and a leg for a replacement ink cartridge.

In fact, a set of official replacement inks could easily cost you more than the printer did in the first place.

Pukka Ink Inc.

The solution is to go onto eBay and buy some unofficial replacement ink cartridges. These cost a fraction of what you'd have to shell out at a computer store, but do almost exactly the same job. For the price of one official cyan cartridge, I can buy six unofficial ones.

The printer isn't happy about this. The minute I go to print anything it wants to establish a connection with its official website to let them know what's going on.

It doesn't get very far. I have security in place and I get tipped off that it's trying to badmouth me to HQ. I press the option that says Don't Allow. The printer knows I've crammed it full of unofficial ink but what's it going to do now…?

The more sophisticated printers have a tiny electronic chip that you have to transfer to each new cartridge to deceive it that it's getting genuinely overpriced cartridges. Presumably at some point in the future they'll work out a way of ensuring that you buy their product, but until that time…

Printer Says "No"

One of the things that my printer likes to do to keep me on my toes is to change the paper setting at random. It always pays to check beforehand. It has a list of papers that it has settings for; these range from plain paper to art paper, to photo paper, to glossy, medium glossy, super glossy, ultra glossy, deluxe glossy, fancy mega glossy and so ridiculously glossy you'll hardly believe it when you see it (which has made the drop-down bar very wide indeed).

After you've printed a photo it has a habit of sneaking back to the plain paper setting, and then for the next ten minutes it drains your inkjet cartridges dry printing out a photo on bog standard white paper that you have to throw away immediately.

You can hear the voice of David Walliams (from the *Little Britain* sketch "Computer Says 'No'") saying, "well you asked for default paper…"

Campaign of Resistance

There are other ways it will try and get back at you for denying it access to its own website. It refuses to give you accurate ink levels when you ask it and will signal that it is low on yellow or magenta just seconds after you have given it a new cartridge. With black it tries a different tactic and reports that there is loads and loads and then runs out in the middle of a document.

Occasionally, it will print out half a picture, blocking off the inkjets for the first six centimetres of the photo but happily wasting ink on printing the remaining 80 per cent of the image.

Sometimes you can print out a black and white document with no colour whatsoever and halfway through it reports that it's run out of yellow.

The only response open to you is to make it jump through all the fault diagnosis hoops – check alignment, clean print-head, check colour nozzles etc. By the time you've whirred and clicked your way through a set of these twice over it's usually ready to behave again.

Then its final act of resistance is to feed in the paper at 15 degrees from horizontal. The more expensive the piece of paper, the more likely it is to do it.

Hey, Photocopier, Fetch!

Photocopiers have come on in leaps and bounds in the last 20 years. Whereas the poor fax machine has withered on the vine of technological progress, the photocopier is with us still, eager to show us what it can do. In the past, if we wanted to jam some paper in a bit of beige machinery then the fax machine was the premier instrument of choice. Today it is the photocopier that rules the roost in the office, having taken on the role of the fax and the printer, while casting a covetous eye on what the scanner can do as well.

Our photocopier is irritatingly eager. When you send something to print, it adopts the persona of a Labrador dog that has just seen you pick up a tennis ball. It activates the receiving trays and they all move up and down to show you how good they are at moving up and down. Then they revert to the position they were before because you only want A4 and not some obscure format like Icelandic A6 (which they're quite capable of doing if you only gave them the chance).

It's not quite as irritating as a muddy-pawed beast jumping up at you and depositing saliva on your trousers, but you know, I bet it would do that as well if it could. It is dying to impress you, if only you'd give it the opportunity to merge a document or insert staples.

Prima Donna

The thing that would impress us most would be if it could run for a period of two days without breaking down. In the past, when we sent documents to a bog standard laser printer, it never broke down. True, it didn't have much memory and if you sent it a long document with pictures then it would think about if for an awfully long time, but it got there in the end. And it never broke down.

The old joke used to be that outside the industrial unit in the business park there was a dedicated parking slot for the photocopier repairman. So, perhaps I should be reassured things haven't changed that much over the years. Now we send our documents to a photocopier/printer and it churns them out with maximum fanfair in no time at all. When it goes wrong, which it inevitably will, a variety of short balding men appear with neat briefcases and a defensive sense of humour. Our photocopier never fails to delight them with a new fault they haven't seen before.

And we're only talking about the black and white photocopier here. The colour photocopier is a total prima donna that requires their strict attendance on a monthly basis. Should someone fail to provide her with the right kind of paper, 100 GSM at the very minimum, then that is a guaranteed paper jam from the moment the "toilet paper" hits her sensitive rollers.

Paper Jam Righter

When you had a boring old laser printer, the paper tray was very close to the printout action. If you got a paper jam you opened the door at the back and yanked out the offending bit of crinkled paper. Paper jams with our modern photocopier printer are a whole lot more involved. There is so much distance between the paper tray and the point of foul-up that you have to spend 40 minutes working out where the offending bit of paper has ended up. There are drawers to be pulled open, flaps to be looked in, whole printing assemblies to be slid out and looked behind.

When you think you've found the offending piece of paper, neatly folded like a Japanese fan in the rollers near the output tray, you slide the machine back together only for it to flash up the message that there's a paper jam elsewhere. By the time you've cleared half of Finland's forests from every compartment, roller, and tray in the thing, 20 people have entered the print queue, meaning you have another 40 minutes till you can print out your document without the machine thinking it's a bit of origami.

Arch-Enemy in a Hand-Knitted Cardigan

There is a kindly old lady in our office, not unlike one of the fairy godmothers in Walt Disney's *Cinderella*, who is the machine's nemesis. She will clog up the print queue with all kinds of bizarre requests, selected inadvertently. She thinks she's printing a standard document but for some reason chooses to print it in U.S. Letter format. When it doesn't print out, she stands and looks at the printer, sighs sadly, then walks away.

The machine makes no allowance for her age. It doesn't realise that she knits her own cardigans or has her hair in a bun. It has got an A4 tray, an A3 tray and anything else it greets with silent incomprehension. You can send U.S. Letter to it all day, it's just going to stand there looking blank. To continue the 'Fetch!' analogy, it's like when you throw a ball and the dog has no idea where it's gone so it just stands there looking at you, hopefully.

Not deterred, our dear old stick goes back to her desk and sends the document again in U.S. Letter format thinking she might not have pressed something properly the first time. When yet again it doesn't emerge she decides she'll leave it. Thus no one in the office can print anything until it's cleared out of the queue.

Occasionally she'll go and get Dale the I.T. guy and ask why something hasn't printed out. Dale will bring up the print queue on the machine and gently point out that the ID of the first five jobs is hers... and why has she chosen the mail merge option...?

She does make marvellous scones, though.

Video Games

'I've suggested to him that it would make it rather quirky if, in the midst of all this classic imagery, you could have them travelling between battles in Austin 1100s. I know it wouldn't be possible to use them in the dense and impenetrable Great Forest of Ajutan, but maybe on the vast plains of Zurethon?'

One really positive thing I can say about video games is that they are going to lessen the incidence of skin cancer somewhere down the line. Left to their own devices children will spend so much time indoors playing them that their exposure to the sun during childhood will be minimal. Their time under that strange golden orb in the sky will probably be limited to the times they were forced into the sunshine on sports days at school and other loathsome occasions when they had to play proper sports that are dependent on real physics and the vagaries of chance, not some pre-programmed sequence written by a computer programmer called Keith in Milton Keynes.

Computer games also keep them from going out and mugging bus-stops and daubing graffiti on old ladies. And if earth were ever to be threatened by killer zombies then most teenagers know how to fight off many different varieties, from your bog standard possessed soul to robot zombies and even to killer Nazi zombies.

A Short History of Evil

As we get more and more digitally enabled, so video games have started to creep into everything we own. To start off with they were limited to a dedicated games console like an Atari or a NES (Nintendo Entertainment System), which brought us Mario and Asteroids and Pacman and Space Invaders. These were heady times. Before then you had to hang out at the pub or find a pier with an arcade and play the game on a massive machine. Suddenly these mind-blowing games were in the home!

Then Sonic arrived with the Sega Mega Drive and

suddenly Sega were the coolest kids on the block. Then we got the Nintendo Game Boy, which took video games out of the front room and into the small sweaty hand. As diversions for small children on long journeys, or interminable lunches in France when you could swear the waiter had emigrated between courses, they were a godsend. But you paid the price for that relief with Duracell batteries.

Then video games transferred to the PC, though the better ones were still on the dedicated consoles like the Sony PlayStation, which then morphed into the PlayStation 2 and had to fight off the Xbox, and then the Xbox360. Microsoft had the brilliant and correct idea that games players tend to be Johnny No Mates and so they hooked up players via the Internet.

Nintendo couldn't beat these two global players at their own game, so they invented another one called the Wii that pretended you could do lots of active stuff while playing video games and not just veg out on the sofa in a sea of empty pizza boxes.

They reinvented the Game Boy as the Nintendo DS, which they tried to get adults to buy by selling games they called "brain training" although adding an "S" to the second word would be more appropriate. While all this was happening, PC graphics cards were getting more and more sophisticated too, especially with the help of the XFi-4B. So the PC got a slice of the market too, especially for the "sophisticated" role-playing games where you had to give yourself a character (or avatar) such as an elf, or an orc.

Not to be outdone, mobile phones loaded games onto their models, which got more and more sophisticated, until Apple gave us the first smartphone where you could buy a ton of different games all intended to rob you of your eyesight. Now we have the iPad and a whole raft of looky-likey tablet PCs that you will be able to play games on.

Before long you will be able to fill in the six minutes of "wasted" time that the microwave is cooking your ready-meal by playing a game on an LCD inserted into its door front.

I'm certainly with the Amish on this one, give them a bowling hoop and send them out into the street.

Zombie Fun

One thing you learn pretty early on is – don't play your children at video games. The moment my son was faster than me around Silverstone in a McLaren MP4-19 I hung up my driving gloves for good. Racing and rally games are good clean wholesome fun, but so many of the games on sale deal with wanton death and destruction.

As someone who reveres what our servicemen did in both World Wars (not to mention the Glorious Gloucesters in Korea) I was horrified to see the casual way kids engaged with battle games. All of a sudden I became very right-on about it.

My wife wanted every shoot-em-up banned from the house but we compromised in that they could have games where they weren't killing other human beings – so were limited to monsters, aliens and attack droids.

When they were older I made them learn the history of D-Day and the Battle for Europe before they were allowed to play the Call of Duty series. They had to sit through *Saving Private Ryan* and the whole series of *Band of Brothers* before they got to run from hedgerow to hedgerow in the bocage of Normandy.

Occasionally, other games would appear and on closer inspection the dim shapes they were firing at seemed like people. "No, they're zombies," was the usual reply.

Keeping It Real

I would like to see a graphic pre-game warning applied to all video games. The kind of trailer that would be introduced by the Grump Republic would run in the same way as adverts before ITV or C4 programmes on catch-up. For programmes you've missed on commercial TV you're obliged to see an advert before you get to watch the programme online. If you want to play what I would consider an obscene game like Grand Theft Auto, which involves carjacking and a lot worse, you would have to sit through real-life photos of the aftermath of a gangland shootout accompanied by the wailing of the victims' relatives. That might dampen the allure of the gangsta lifestyle.

Get A Life-Craft!

The most pernicious example of the video game, though, is the life-sucking MMORPG. Yes, it's even got an unfathomable acronym. This stands for Massively Multi-player Online Role Playing Game (sic). How can you have something that's "massively multi-player"? One of my sons got hooked on World of Warlock and it was like the Moonie organisation for video gamers. It began to take over his life. One important aspect of the game is "the guild". People form themselves into guilds and guild members have to be online at agreed times of the evening to take part in raids where they battle monsters, wage war against the trolls or capture hill forts held by orcs.

I didn't at this stage tell him that a guild traditionally contained members with a discernible skill.

There is a plethora of games that have ripped off the imagery and vocabulary of Tolkien's *Lord of the Rings*. They are populated with dwarves, elves, orcs, trolls, warlords, mystical wizards and fearsome creatures in the mould of Tolkien's "Balrog". This is a world of medieval weaponry and technology where men fight dragons on horseback and fire catapults and ballisters.

I've suggested to him that it would make it rather quirky if, in the midst of all this classic imagery, you could have them travelling between battles in Austin 1100s. I know it wouldn't be possible to use them in the dense and impenetrable Great Forest of Ajutan, but maybe on the vast plains of Zurethon? The warlord Croll and his famous axe Skullsplitter could arrive in an Austin 1100 to put the usurping Silesians to the sword.

Unfortunately, he hasn't taken the bait and suggested it in a guild forum. I knew they all had specific roles, so I asked him what role he played in the guild and he told me he was a healer. This means he stays to the rear when they go out to fight and has to tend to the wounds of the valiant warriors as they attempt to take a bridge off a motley band of dwarf mercenaries.

He's got to work his way up to frontline duties in the guild's vital raging and pillaging work. To do this he's got to impress the Guild Master. The Guild Master is the person who organises this band of multi-skilled battle veterans and decides the strategy and sets the guild's objectives. We

124

discovered that my son's Guild Master worked for a well-known supermarket collecting trolleys and wasn't best pleased when he overheard Mrs Grump opining, "he sounds like a paedophile".

All of a sudden my son found that his services as a healer were no longer required in the guild, which was great news. Unfortunately, he found another guild soon after.

Say 'Oui' to Wii

Guess what they call the Nintendo Wii in France? Well, actually, they still call it the Nintendo Wii... which surely must cause problems somewhere along the line. Especially if they pronounce it the same as oui.

The Nintendo Yes sounds a very positive branding exercise for a quasi-sporting product, but they might not say it that way.

I bring this up purely because their pronunciation of the word wi-fi is so hilarious. We already have hi-fi, so wi-fi isn't too much of a step for us.

The French don't talk about "le wi-fi", they talk about "le wee-fee". Yes, the wee-fee, she is at home, feeding the French poodle, FeeFee, before taking 'er out for a walk and ze peepee. Later she will watch *The X-Files* on television because she adores the scee-fee.

For all I know the perfidious French will have taken a different linguistic route for the Nintendo Wii and placed the emphasis on the two 'i's. So instead of Nintendo "wee" they'll say Nintendo "wi-i". It would be fantastic to hear 60 million French people talking with a Geordie accent – why aye – and I've no doubt they could (60 million Brits can speak with a Jamaican accent simply by saying the phrase 'beer can sandwich'), it's getting them to watch football matches in winter with their tops off and drink Newcastle Brown ale that might be the difficult part. They'd have to rename it *Bierre Brun de Nouvelle-Chateau*.

Gadgets

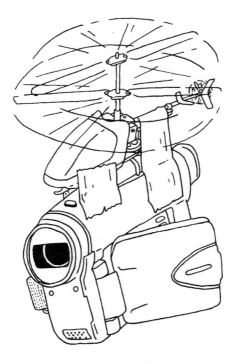

'You can leave your paperback on a sunlounger while you go to lunch. Leave your Kindle there and you'll find it's either been swiped or the sun has done interesting and imaginative things to the black plastic in 30°C heat.'

Inspect a Gadget

One of the best gadgets I ever owned came to me as a freebie back in the dim distant 1990s. It had the Williams' F1 team branding on the front and you stuck it on the dashboard of your car. It was a beautifully designed, small black box, with a row of dummy LEDs, purposeful curves and edges. In looks and positioning it resembled one of those radar trap detector devices that men with mullets and Porsche 911s had before the days of SatNav. Everybody who got into my car immediately fixed eyes upon it and wanted to know what mischief this mysterious little box got up to. Surely something which looked that "gadgety" did something extremely interesting…?

It was an air freshener.

Their profound disappointment illuminates the whole vicarious thrill of the gadget. People love a gadget. When they discover that what they thought was a gadget is actually no more than a fancily clad "traffic light" they're left feeling almost bereft.

Don't Fondle My Kindle

One of the growing gadgets to have is the e-reader, the most prominent of which is the Amazon Kindle. Compared to the iPad or a tablet PC it's a one-trick pony. It's like comparing the old Sony Walkman to an MP3 player. The Walkman was around a lot earlier but the MP3 player was way funkier.

The Kindle has been around longer than the iPad, but we all know which is sexier. Even if the Kindle is a lot cheaper. (Apple nerds might point out that the much earlier Newton notebook wasn't so far away.) For a start the name is atrocious – kindle is a bit like Kinder Surprise and not too far away from fondle. "Would you like to fondle my Kindle?"*

Whoever thought up the name probably had a hand in failing to rebrand the Ford Pinto for the Brazilian market. Pinto is slang in Brazil for the male genitals.

*Incidentally, if the publishers of this book finally do a deal with Amazon and make it available for the Kindle, then I would just like to say I have had a conversion on the road to Damascus and I think they're marvellous things. What value!

The Pros and Cons of the E-reader

There are positive things to be said for the Kindle as well as negative... so there's only one way to sort this out:

Kindle Versus the Paperback

Against: You can leave your paperback on a sunlounger while you go to lunch. Leave your Kindle there and you'll find it's either been swiped or the sun has done interesting and imaginative things to the black plastic in 30°C heat.

For: You can get more than enough reading material onto a Kindle to last a lifetime, so no regretting that you only packed three paperbacks instead of four.

Against: Lend anyone your downloaded copy of the latest Sebastian Faulks and that's copyright theft. Lend someone the paperback and it's an act of kindness.

For: It can be read in all kinds of low-light situations.

Against: ...providing the batteries last. Imagine how annoying it would be to get within four pages of the end on a long flight home and then...

For: No need to buy all those shelving units from IKEA that trap and clog up your chi energy. A single Kindle is very minimalist, very Feng Shui.

Against: You'll have to find another use for the library in the West Wing.

For: It'll be one up for you if you're the first person to have one in Book Club.

Against: When everyone gets one, you'll have to call it Kindle Club.

Gadget Culture

If there is one single programme that has helped foster our worship of gimmicky old toot then it is C5's *The Gadget Show*. I mean who hasn't got the latest remote controlled helicopter cam...? The programme is presented by one of those hairless Siamese cats in oversize geeky glasses. There is middle-aged beauty, Suzi Perry, a cheeky upstart called Ortis, plus a token blonde and a token older person – presumably to show us that both these demographics can understand and use gadgets, no matter what the real-life perception. Together they look like the IT Department Christmas Lunch.

Now, I wouldn't mind taking a bet that if you stood outside a branch of Maplin of a Saturday afternoon, you would get a far more homogenous group of individuals stepping through. We wouldn't be talking about the cutting edge of men's fashion. And their preferred method of rain avoidance would always be anoraks.

Admiring the Bentley

Naturally my sons adore it. And I have to say I have a sneaking admiration too, basically because the one that looks like a Siamese cat in glasses has got a tremendous amount of bottle. He is the John Noakes of *The Gadget Show*. He will jump off the top of Nelson's column to compare two hand-held altimeters (the latest gadget you just can't be without).

I also like the idea that Jon Bentley – the unashamedly posh and unashamedly old guy – has a place on the presenting team. Too many TV presenters want to be your mate and he never could be, he would always be the sniffy neighbour looking over your fence and telling you to stake your peonies. It's probably all an act and in reality he's got a thick Black Country accent and says things like, "what's up, duck?" But the BBC would be far too right-on to employ him for anything except the *Last Night of the Proms* or the *Antiques Roadshow*. Yet he's great on *The Gadget Show*. Like some prep school housemaster trying to make science interesting for the boys.

Stuff and Nonsense

Even more irritating is the gadget magazine *Stuff*. *Stuff* is like Winnie the Pooh, full of fluff. What's more they don't have confidence in their own editorial strengths. Why don't they put a gadget on the front of their gadget-based magazine? With *Practical Caravanning*, you don't get a lissome model dressed in something tight and rubbery draped across the latest four-berth Alpine Wanderer. You get a caravan.

With *Cage and Aviary Birds*, you don't get a Penelope Cruz lookalike struggling to stay inside a Size 8 bikini, you get a parakeet. So why is it that *Stuff* and their wannabe rival, *T3*, have to revert to the sexist sell…? Perhaps that's where Maplin are going wrong. They could attract far more customers into the store if they put up some life-size models of Megan Fox and Cheryl Cole in the window.

The Spy in Your Bin

Today we live in a world of gadgets. The cost and size of silicon chips has come down so much that they can be inserted into everything. We almost ended up with a computer chip in the bottom of our wheelie bins to spy on what we were chucking out. How that was going to work I'm not entirely sure – the only thing it could tell the binmen was maybe the weight and who it belonged to. Unless it had some weird sensing device they devised from all those Mars probes, which could analyse the chemical make-up of matter in a one-metre radius.

Or maybe the new wheelie bin is going to be a mini MRI scanner that sends back complex pictures of our rubbish via a satellite link to a newly appointed Rubbish Tsar.

I'd be quite happy to pay for what I chuck in the bin, but before all that happens we need to impose a rubbish tax on supermarkets. There should be an unnecessary packaging tax levied on them first. We can't choose whether to take a product home with or without the packaging, so get them to pay. They make monstrous levels of profit and enjoy squeezing the living daylights out of farmers and other suppliers, so let them take the pain.

Digital Cameras

'It's almost impossible to take a bad picture these days, but I try my hardest.'

Here's something it's very difficult to get grumpy about. As a keen amateur photographer my artistic horizons have been extended by the CMOS sensor and others of its ilk. There are so many pluses to a digital camera that only the most dyed-in-the-wool unyielding curmudgeon could find anything nasty to say about them. So, here we go...

Needless Histograms

Occasionally when I press the wrong button on the camera there is some weird graph that comes up at the side. What are they all about, then? How many photographers look at them and think, "Hmm, my cyan to magenta balance was a bit awry there..." when all that matters is that the photo is framed correctly. Nobody's going to be quibbling about the accurate representation of Auntie Hilda's peach cardie when she's got her eyes shut.

That kid of guff is only on the camera as a sop to camera reviewers, the 0.005 per cent of the population that know what any of it means.

You Can't Take a Poor Picture

The histogram is one part of the arms/space/technology race to make cameras more sophisticated, more intuitive, more adaptable. Some of the features they have put on cameras you wouldn't dream were possible – face recognition and focusing, the ability to spot familiar faces in the frame and focus on them. (With certain members of my extended family I'd quite like "face blanking and blurring" where they were thrown out of focus in favour of the background.)

With all kinds of devices to balance the light, image stabilisation to stop camera shake, automatic flash and adaptive ISO to allow pictures to be taken in very low levels of light, it's very hard to take a poor picture these days. I can still find ways but it's getting more and more tricky.

What is forever creeping up, though, is the size of the images. My first digital camera recorded pictures at 1.3 megapixels. These days it would be hard to find a mobile phone with a camera that small. The next one was 6 megapixels and my current model does 12. Next time I change, it will be for a model that does 18 megapixels. Very soon we will all be taking pictures that could be blown up and used on the side of a bus. If indeed they want pictures of "interesting beehives I have spotted".

The consequences of this are that hard drives need to become bigger and email inboxes get easily swamped.

Now I know that there will always be buttons on cameras where you can change between "Fine" quality and "Medium" quality, but who wants medium when you can have fine?

Do You Want to Delete?

The delete buttons on digital cameras have been idiot-proofed to the point where it's easier to fire a Polaris missile than delete images. The camera is wary of allowing you access to its horde of precious pixels. "Do you want to delete? No, seriously, do you want to go ahead and delete…? Now you're absolutely sure you want to go ahead and delete, because I'm only going to give you one final warning after this. Okay, this is the last time I'm going to say anything, but after this, all those pictures that you took are going to be gone, now you haven't got any last-minute worries, because I'm going to delete…"

Perhaps in the future they will make a camera for super-indecisive photographers who want a kind of PC recycle bin arrangement. Photos would be put into a kind of purgatory, before either ascending into the heaven of the PC picture file or crashing into the flames of hell and permanent deletion.

What a Card!

One of the great benefits of the digital camera is that it allows you to take so many more pictures than when you had roll film cameras and every image had to count. Given that most memory cards will allow you to take between 100 and 1,000 hi-res photos it's still surprising how many people will take single shots of a once-in-a-lifetime moments and leave it at that. The immense joy of the digital camera is to take too many shots and then delete the bad ones afterwards. Less isn't more with photography, unless you're eye-to-eye with a rock ape and that extra shot will see the camera change hands.

The basic idea behind the memory card is that you buy one, take photos on it, download the photos to your PC, delete photos off the card, and start again. I thought this didn't need much explanation.

My father-in-law had a fully functioning PC when he swapped his circa 1964 Nikon (which even Nikon had run out of spare parts for) for his first digital camera, so I assumed he'd understand the principles of a memory card.

After about a year and a half I asked him to show me some of his images on his PC. He said he hadn't downloaded them yet. He'd amassed 17 memory cards all full of photos and never deleted one of them…

Even when I showed him how to download them to his PC I suspect he didn't wipe them and re-use them; he comes from a generation that likes something tangible to hang onto and these 17 memory cards are his negatives. Given what's happened to at least one of our friends' PCs, it's not entirely a system without merit.

I'm Feeling Lucky

You can be a very lazy photographer nowadays as well. What you don't capture properly at the time you can correct afterwards. I know in some quarters Google are seen as the evil empire, taking over the Google Earth, but their Picasa image editing software is free and a joy to use.

It can sharpen, crop, flip, level, balance colour and contrast, highlight and shadow. It also has an "I'm feeling lucky" button, like on most Google applications. I tried it on some of the photos I'd taken but it didn't turn the wife's mother into a glamorous granny. Though where it got that paper bag with the eyeholes I'll never know…

Koniophobia

One of the few drawbacks of the digital camera system is the fear of dust on your sensor. Great big knobby chunks of dust on your sensor are going to spell doom and so if you want to change to a telephoto lens you have to be absolutely thorough in changing them over. I don't get near to "absolutely thorough" in any of my dealings with technology and I usually want to change lenses on the touchline of the school rugby pitch on a howling wet November afternoon. I have to announce loudly, "I'm going to change lenses", otherwise the furtive rummaging inside my jacket might look particularly suspicious.

Technology Creep

'Stand by for the new technologically enhanced
coffee mug that gives you a digital read-out
of everything from caffeine content to where
the beans were picked!'

Gradually, technology is creeping into more and more areas of our lives. And it's not going to go away...unless it's a wristwatch.

Digital Reverts to Mechanical

Our children are the digital natives and we are the reluctant digital migrants. Though sometimes I like to think that I am a digital vagrant. I have migrated but I'm angry about it.

In a short space of time cameras have gone digital, communication has gone digital, TV and radio are in the process of going digital, so it's nice to see that one area has flirted with digital and gone back to old fashioned mechanical – the wristwatch. People have tried digital watches, found they haven't liked them, and stuck with 500-year-old technology.

Ironically, it's the one device that every science fiction writer thought would be blazing the trail of gadgetry – we were going to have watch cameras, watch videophones, watch organisers, watch calculators, but in the end they're just watches.

The New X-ray Machines

Something along the same lines as an MRI scanner is the body-scanning machine that they've introduced to some airports. These are the ones that give a particularly accurate picture of your anatomy when you walk through them. Many people have objected to them because they are quite revealing. Well, very revealing. But that's the price you pay for safe and fast international travel. If you object strongly, take the ferry. I can assure you that there are none at Portsmouth or Dover.

If it means one less bomb exploding in an airplane and one less planeload of people falling 33,000 feet to their doom then I am for it, and sod the civil liberties aspect. You don't turn up at the hospital for an operation and say, "Nurse, I'm rather keen to keep my clothes on for most of this."

And pity the poor monitors who have to sit there all day staring at a succession of flabby bodies coming through. Generally speaking, international terrorists don't work out at the gym or have the curves or long legs of catwalk models. That's why they become terrorists, because there was always someone kicking sand in their face.

CCTV Frenzy

You occasionally come across articles that say we are the most surveilled society in the world. Attached to it is some liberal wishy-washy opinion piece mentioning erosion of freedom and big brother watching over us and citing the 700,000 CCTV cameras that the UK possesses. In fact, there was a report by a chief constable last year pointing out that there had been a bit of a mistake when calculating the number of CCTV cameras. It turns out some statistical genius had worked out the number of CCTV cameras per head in London and then extrapolated it for the rest of the population.

When the figures were adjusted to include less developed areas he found that there were more likely to be 400,000 CCTV cameras. I was outraged. Why aren't there 700,000? I found that figure very reassuring.

I am more than relaxed with the fact that I may pass 60 to 70 CCTV cameras in any given day. I'm not doing anything wrong, so I don't mind. Nobody's going to get a vicarious thrill of watching me go into the newsagent and buy a Fry's Chocolate Cream instead of a Twix. This is the bonus of technology making us safer and technology making for a just society.

When violence flares outside a nightclub at 2am, as it invariably does, there could be a long court argument as to whether an aggrieved punter was dropkicked out of the door by an overzealous bouncer (very much like the TV kids in *TV Comic* – anybody remember that?). The CCTV camera cuts to the chase and saves so much argument.

The zenith of this was the cat-in-the-wheelie-bin CCTV incident. Up until the point that Mrs Mary Bale pushed tabby cat "Lola" into a wheelie bin and shut the lid, the neighbours probably thought that Darryl and Stephanie Andrews-Mann were a bit strange for recording the front of their garden. When the cat-loving world saw the footage they were outraged and suddenly all that electricity was worth it.

Lycra Lout TV

And talking of arguments, people can misuse camcorders, too. There is now a growing wave of Lycra louts: cyclists who strap a sports action camcorder to their helmet to record the misdeeds of motorists who cut them up in traffic. That's cut them up after the cyclist has jumped three sets of red lights, ignored several Give Way signs and taken a short cut the wrong way down a one-way street.

True, there are a lot of dangerous drivers out there, but their number pales into insignificance compared to the sheer volume of dangerous cyclists. And I should know, I cycle to work.

If I stop for a red light and there are four cyclists behind me, one is likely to stop and the other three will go through. One will carry on at speed as though there was no light there at all, one will actually slow down to look and see if there is any traffic likely to endanger them and the third will go through very slowly, inch forward, then take the plunge.

I'm quite happy for cyclists with cycle-cams to record their journeys to work, but if anything happens, they have to show the whole of the footage, not just the 3 per cent of the journey when they were in the right and for a fleeting moment somebody else was in the wrong.

Car Tech

Not surprisingly there is a lot of technology that has gone into motoring in the last 20 years. There was a time when a trip computer was the white heat of technology in a showroom model. Not any more. These days there are computers controlling and monitoring everything: ride height, fuel flow, tyre pressure, suspension travel, traction control.

McLaren set the standard with their 1992 supercar, the F1. When it broke down it would telephone back to McLaren HQ and tell the technicians what was wrong with it. Well, not quite, but it was equipped with a modem. When you pay £500,000 for a car you really shouldn't expect anything less.

These days your local garage has the ability to plug any car into a laptop to work out what's wrong with the engine. What was once the optional extra of the privileged few is now a standard item on the cheapest of mass-produced models. Though I doubt Tata will send out a helicopter to repair one of their £2,000 Nano cars when the plugs get oily. McLaren would.

Parking Sensor

Parking can be a nadgy business, especially if you're of the fairer sex. I don't mean to turn this into a diatribe against women drivers or a patronising aside, because, bless you, you're only doing your best. Men can do very few things better than women; evict spiders, kick footballs hard, unscrew the tops off jars... and park vehicles. That's about it. And now the rear-parking sensor has emasculated us even further by aiding that role.

At least that's what I thought when we bought my wife a car with a rear parking sensor. This device bleeps inside the car, a little like the bleep you get when a lorry reverses. Except as you get closer to the vehicle behind the bleeps get closer and closer together to indicate the distance. When you are almost touching it is almost one continuous bleep.

One day I came home and as I pulled into the drive I noticed that the rear of her fairly new car was bent inwards. Naturally I asked who had hit her. I had to couch this in fairly careful terms because she is quite sensitive to criticism of her driving style. It's a bit like when my daughter was six years old and came home with a painting of a lovely lake with green ducks. I asked her why the ducks were green, "ducks are white aren't they?"

"They've been sitting on duckweed, Daddy!" was the answer hissed at me. She had reasoned it all out, how DARE I question the logic of her picture.

It turned out that my wife had been reversing into a space, the device had done its job and emitted its siren cry of a continuous bleep, but my wife had ignored it. She knew that there wasn't anything at bumper level and thought it was a fault in the sensor. Then the branch, which was higher up than the bumper, smacked into the back of the car and dented the rear door.

It was the sensor's fault.

Completely Keyless

One of the other star turns of her new (but dented) car was the lack of an ignition key. Instead of a physical key that went into an ignition, it had a Bluetooth device that told the car when the "key" was present. This was the same key that locked the doors and turned the alarm on and off etc.

This thing was so smart that you didn't even have to wave it anywhere near the steering column. The car would simply seek the reassurance of the key's presence in my wife's handbag and allow the car to be started. This worked out fine when she was driving.

When I'm driving her into the town centre and, to save time, drop her off outside M&S before joining the queue for the car park, we hit a major snag. I'm now in the car with no ignition key. She's gone off with the ignition key in her bag. The car, although requiring the key to be present to start up, is quite happy to keep running when the ignition key is taken away. Should it stall I can't restart it. Should I need to lock it or alarm it I can't, because the key is now in the middle of cheap summer tops in Primark.

It's supposed to save time and be convenient, but as we must have done this on three separate occasions now, I can't really see the convenience.

The Ford Bossy Boots

There is so much more coming, though. The new cars in the Ford range have got an optional low-speed safety system. You know the situation, you can be trundling along in stop-start traffic at slow speed when your eyes are inadvertently drawn to the latest Wonderbra billboard. It's not your fault, these breasts are 11 feet across. Just as your eyes are temporarily diverted, the car in front brakes, you keep on trundling and crunch! The Ford system will spot this and if you're not going to stop, the car will take matters into its own hands and brake for you.

That's not all. There is a system that spots when you're wandering out of lane by monitoring your position in relation to the white lines. If you cross the line without indicating, then it gives a great big tut and steers you back. Or it can alert you to the fact by putting a great big vibration through the steering wheel and letting you steer back yourself.

You'll be able to buy one of the bossiest cars on the road. Front-facing cameras will flash up speed warning signs that you've ignored. It will also monitor your driving style to check signs of fatigue and advise you to stop driving.

Its pièce de résistance, though, is the parallel parking system. Using its full array of rear, side and front sensors all you have to do is pull up to an empty space, take your hands off the wheel and press accelerator and brake. It'll do all the steering into the space for you.

Very soon there'll be a Ford that asks you to mind your own business and sit in the back. And don't mess around with the cigarette lighter!

'My SatNav Tried to Kill Me'

From time to time – but mostly a slow news day – you will read a story along the lines of "My SatNav tried to kill me". The gist of the story will be that some driver slavishly followed his SatNav's instructions when it advised him to turn right into a ravine and he managed to slam on the anchors at the very last minute and avoid certain catastrophe. I'd be quite happy for them to keep on going and not muddy the gene pool any further.

SatNavs are on the whole very benign bits of technology, kindly assistants only trying to do their best. Ninety-eight per cent of the time they are a real help, it's just that cranky 2 per cent of the time when the software hits a glitch that you have to watch out for.

We were travelling up from the South of France one Easter on the *péage* or toll motorway, anxious to get to Eurotunnel on time (because we know what chaos can ensue when you don't). All of a sudden our SatNav directed us off the 80 mph *péage* onto a local side road. We queued up and paid for our ticket. Then we pottered along a local B-road for about five miles behind a tractor.

Then it directed us back onto the *péage* at the next entry point. Hein?

We queued to take a ticket, got onto the motorway again and then were stuck behind the same soot-belching, wheezing, asthmatic trucks of an hour previously. After hauling out the Michelin roadmap we realised what the SatNav had done. Because there was a kink in the auto-route, it had spotted that in terms of distance-as-the-crow-flies, taking us off the *péage* saved us a whole kilometre in distance travelled. But added half an hour onto our journey time.

How we laughed.

Ticket to Writhe

Unfamiliar parking ticket machines can also be a source of great techno consternation. It helps if I can have my first "go" without a line of people behind. The eyes of a queue of frustrated Saturday shoppers, all anxious to get their car parking paid before they tip over into the next hour can burrow like lasers into the back of your head when you're fumbling in your pockets for the two pound coins you think you know you have. Especially if the machine spits both of them out when they're inserted.

Such has been the hike in the price of parking that more and more are taking credit cards, which makes things a lot easier…at a cost.

Ticket to Hythe

The same applies to an even greater extent for ticket machines at Tube stations where you have to make a choice, not just pay what is due. The pressure is ramped up because there are many people behind you who know exactly what they want and exactly which buttons to press while you are staring at it doing your best Goofy impression, "Aw go-o-o-o-sh, this thing looks ar-fully com-per-licated".

But at least if your bumbling incompetence makes them miss their Tube, there'll be another one along in 10 minutes. Try getting to grips with the ticket machine at your local railway station where there are infinitely more choices, only one machine, and if you miss this train there won't be another for 30 minutes. That's real pressure.

Try fouling up for five minutes, then turning to the queue with a chuckle and saying, "I bet even Frank Spencer would have got a ticket by now. Ha ha ha." You're not going to get a laugh.

Das Ticket

The most fearsomely complicated ticket machine I ever encountered was at Frankfurt Airport. I only wanted to go to Frankfurt main railway station but I was fearful of getting a ticket to the Ryan Air version of Frankfurt station, which was probably close to the Austrian border.

It had what seemed like 80 separate buttons, all with small German writing on. Thankfully there were four of the machines, so me stood in front doing my usual, "Awww heck" for 10 minutes didn't seem to bother anyone. In the end I pressed what I thought was the ticket to the Hauptbahnhof and got a café latte with sugar.

A nice German man helped me press the correct one. I ought to point out that German people are exceptionally friendly and really keen to assist. Later on in the trip I stopped and took out a street map for what must have been a nanosecond before a German voice said, "Can I help you…?"

Unexpected Item in the Bagging Area

Contrary to what you might expect, I love the challenge of a supermarket self-checkout machine. It's a little bit Las Vegas, isn't it? You get to press a few buttons, lights flash, you put money in, a voice talks to you, and you get back much less than you started with. Only with the bonus that you get to walk away with your own shopping. There may not be a quarter scale model of Big Ben, two-ton Texans in sneakers and dancing girls but it's a little bit of razzmatazz. All right, maybe not Las Vegas, how about Margate?

Anyone who's encountered one will no doubt have heard the announcement, "Unexpected item in the bagging area." I'm not entirely sure what kind of expectations the machine has of what you are going to stick in its bagging area, but it gets surprised on a regular basis. Indeed, the great point of conflict seems to be in the bagging area; you can also have a "bagging alert" or receive the instruction, "return item to bagging area". It will accept the grottiest notes and the grubbiest coins, but fool around with the bagging area and it's going to let you know.

Sometimes, if you've been fumbling around with something in your shopping basket and failed to scan a product for a while it will say in an ever-so-slightly sarcastic way, "Do you want to continue…?"

Thankfully, where I use one there are four machines, one of which is never working, so there's no great pressure. The only thing I really have against it is that it fails to recognise that I'm over 18.

Doctor Tech

The doctor's practice hasn't been immune to the spread of technology either. Now when I arrive at the surgery to see the doctor, I don't need to talk to the receptionist, I can go straight to the touch-screen check-in device and register my presence. It's like the easiest pub quiz game in the world – a choice of male or female, followed by your date of birth.

This is a good way to start clearing out some of the coffin dodgers who tend to clog up doctors' waiting rooms – make them operate some technology before they come in with their unnecessary visit. That'll whittle them down. Those two questions are hardly enough…

The other bit of good news is that with computerised notes doctors can transfer them and access them remotely, and it's all legible. Everyone is always banging on about confidentiality of doctors' notes, as though what was written on them was really interesting. I couldn't give a stuff who reads my notes. I don't believe society will shun me if they found out I had pyloric stenosis as a baby. Society has many more reasons to shun me than that. And with the spate of embarrassing bodies' programmes on television we really have seen it all already.

DIY Tickets

One of the great boons of technology and the universality of home computers is the ability to create and print out tickets ourselves. Let me ask you something. The first time you printed out your own airline e-ticket – did you think it was going to work? I have to admit that 20 per cent of me thought it wasn't. How could you possibly cross the Atlantic on the strength of a six- or seven-figure reference number…? It all seemed so casual.

E-tickets or DIY tickets could be used even more than they are now. I went to a music concert where you printed your own ticket and the guy on the door scanned the barcode. Not only did it verify I had paid to enter, it would verify that I was in the building. There was no need to be sent anything in the post that could have gone missing en route or required a signature.

So why aren't they used more often? Surely the members of the stub-tearers' union could be persuaded to retrain and use a scanning gun. Or is it that the ticket agencies like levying a hefty mark-up via their booking fee and if you do it all online you can hardly justify the charge…?

Scoring An Own Goal – Or Is It…?

One thing where technology should be creeping in but has been resolutely resisted is football. By the time you are reading this I would hope that goal-line technology had been adopted by that stone age organisation (or mafia syndicate, depending which way you like to look at it) FIFA. Why would you even need to trial a system to work out if it was a good idea? You would have thought the embarrassment of such a blatantly disallowed goal in the England vs Germany game in the 2010 World Cup would have helped throw the switch. Frank Lampard's shot was so far over the line it was virtually in the crowd behind the goal, but the referee and linesman didn't see it.

It would have taken them twenty seconds to run over to a monitor at the side of the pitch and confirm the fact, but no, that would break up the game. Players falling down to the ground and feigning injury is fine, you can stop the game for that. But stopping it for a game-changing decision is unthinkable.

Cricket Goes Techno

It's bizarre when you think that cricket, a sport that is often viewed as stuffy and rooted in tradition has the most modern and technological of electronic aids now to confirm umpires' decisions (and occasionally reverse them). There are video cameras to determine hotspots on the bat to see if the batsmen nicked a catch. They have HawkEye cameras to determine the line of the ball to see if it would have hit the stumps from a bowler's delivery. That's in addition to the video replays to see if someone was run out or not.

These innovations are all part of the new Umpire Decision Review System and it is a fantastic improvement, because commentators and pundits don't spend their time moaning about what might have happened.

If you watch Big Ears on *Match of the Day* then often, all he and his panel of barely articulate monkeys wants to talk about is the decisions the referee has got wrong. Managers are interviewed after the game and they complain bitterly about the refereeing. It gives them the perfect excuse for why they failed to do their job. Pity the poor referee who is being judged on decisions he has to make in the blink of an eye while viewers at home are shown the incident again and again, in HD, in slow motion and from four different angles.

If they actually used technology sensibly and had decision reviews on game-changing decisions, such as sendings off and disallowed goals, the same way they do in cricket, rugby, American football, F1, tennis etc., then the fig leaf of poor refereeing would be taken away from a lot of whining overpaid football managers.

The Rise of the Mindless Statistic

Another area of techno creep in sport is the emergence of 'the mindless statistic'. I always thought this was the province of American sport such as baseball and American football, where they like to tell you how many yards a player has run per carry, per game, per season, like it was going to make your day. This is seeping into football where at the end of the game you can find out how many completed passes a team made, how many shots on-target they had, how many shots off-target and how many corners they failed to take advantage of.

Very soon we'll have the average velocity of the ball during the game, the number of throw-ins, distance of throw-in, number of headers, number of passes between left-footed players, number of spits, average distance of spit, number of chews a manager makes in the first half compared to the second. All great, great statistics.

Perhaps the BBC will also caption the number of times one of their football pundits says that "football is a results business".

Formula One, Fifteen, Seven, Nine

And talking about mindless statistics, look no further than the Formula One coverage.

These days staring at the TV screen while an F1 race is in progress is enough to give you a headache. In the good old days, when the laconic delivery of James Hunt let you know exactly what he thought about each and every driver, it was the high-pitched buzz of Murray Walker that gave you the headache.

Now it's an endless stream of information run along the bottom of the screen, up the side of the screen, and for the in-car footage a simulated steering wheel that gives you gear selection, braking, KERS usage and revs. It's like keeping an eye on two stock market tickers at the same time as driving a car and watching sport. Exhausting. No pun intended.

Grumpy Glossary

In the sea of confusion that is the technical universe, let our comprehensive glossary calm your fears with some helpful user-friendly explanations.

Analog – The way it was before digital and all the information was a continuous stream, not made up of binary ones and zeroes. For example, a record player is analog, a CD player is digital. A VCR is analog, a DVD is digital. FM radio is analog and Digital radio is listened to by seven people.

Android – The latter half of the phrase "Park and Ride" as described by a West-Midlander. Less commonly used to describe the Operating System employed in non-Apple smartphones.

Apple – Synonym for overpriced.

Avatars – Characters created for roleplay games by people who really should get out more.

Bandwith – The amount of data you can send down a cable at any one time, usually measured in bps (bits per second). Think of it as a waste pipe where the "b" stands for "bigjobs". The higher the number you can flush away per second, the better the system.

Beta version – The excuse that software developers use when their new programme crashes and burns. They are 98 per cent sure it's finished but there's this nagging fear they've forgotten something, so they release the beta version and wait for some supernerd to point out their mistake.

Bitmap – When you blow up a phone pic far too big and straight lines become steppy lines.

BitTorrent – What your kids use to download illegal movies at speed before you realise that they're slowing down the Internet connection.

Blog – Short for weblog. Something unemployed or retired people do to convince themselves they still have a purpose in life. Most have the lifespan of the average hamster with heart problems.

Blu-ray – Astonishing quality, astonishing expense; the movie format that bridges the gap between DVDs and the next big thing we will all have to buy.

Bluetooth – System used for short-range wireless transmissions, but can pass through walls, unlike infrared, which sometimes has a job passing through air.

Boot – Used with "up". To boot up the computer is to start the computer. You boot out the computer when it won't boot up.

Browser – Internet browser programmes like Internet Explorer (IE), Google Chrome or Buffalo Mozilla.

Byte – Consists of eight bits. Think of it as a take-away pizza.

Cache – Think of it as a larder full of recently downloaded bits of information that you can snack on if you feel like it.

CAD – Computer Aided Design, as exemplified by absolute bounder Terry Thomas.

CCD – It stands for Charged Coupled Device, something that converts light into digital images for digital cameras and videos.

CCS – Band led by hugely influential bluesman Alexis Korner. Had a hit with *Tap Turns on the Water*.

Clock speed – Like a speedometer for the computer chip or processor at the heart of your computer. Affected by the bus speed and the cache size. Obviously.

Computer file – Someone who likes computers.

Cursor – The pointer on your computer that is directed by your mouse, which always gives the first indication that a) Your screen has frozen or b) The cable has come out.

Cyberspace – A virtual space, where the Wurzels go to drink.

DDR-SDRAM – The Porsche 911 of memory.

Defragment – De tiny bit dat's left.

Desktop – Anything that's kicking about on your computer screen when you first boot up.

Dongle – Something you plug into your laptop or desktop PC to give it Wi-Fi compatibility. Also, it's a technique pioneered by Dirk Diggler in soft-core porn movies.

Dual Core – Basically two processors are better than one, but having a dual core as opposed to a single core may not double the speed of some operations because many programmes are not configured to take advantage of duel-core processing. Not even if you have a dongle.

Edutainment – Something that is neither educational nor entertaining but needs a bit of a boost. Hey presto! Edutainment. Probably thought up by an Imagineer.

Ethernet – A network created by computers linked together with LAN (Local Area Network) cables. Considering the ether was space and heaven in Greek mythology you'd think the nerds might have saved this term up for some kind of wireless network.

Excel – Spreadsheet programme that always goes off one side of the page and never prints properly.

External Hard Drive – Extra memory to back up your precious photo files and video clips, which plugs into your PC, usually through a USB port.

FAT32 – In computing FAT is beautiful, FAT is happy, FAT is short for File Allocation Table. FAT32 tucks away all your files and knows where they all are.

File extension – The bit after the full-stop that tells you what kind of computer file you're dealing with, such as jpg, pdf or doc. In the early days of PCs versus Macs it was like the Montagues versus the Capulets when you were trying to open a Mac-generated file on a PC and vice versa.

Firmware – Software written on something that is really solid, like a tree, a rock or, more typically, a hard drive.

Flash – He only had 15 minutes to save the world, but he did it. Adobe Flash is useless in defeating Ming the Merciless but it does help run small animations on websites. It's always a good idea to be Flash-equipped.

Floppy disk – A computer technology so old, they were mentioned in the Norse Sagas. The first floppy disks of 1969 held a whopping 80kb. By 1987 we got the High Density 3.5-inch floppy that could hold an enormous 1.44 megabytes. But were we satisfied…?

Gigabyte – Taken from the Greek word "giga" meaning giant, a gigabyte is roughly 1,000 times bigger than a megabyte, but 1,000 times smaller than a terabyte. Terabyte is derived from the Greek word "teras", meaning monster. As digital cameras demand more and more storage in the future, we will have to move up to even bigger, barely conceivable units of measurement, such as the Greek Debt-abyte.

Hard Disk – The component of your computer that will pack up first, usually 30 minutes before you back up your files with an external hard drive.

HD – This could mean Hard Disk, or it could mean High Definition, or it could mean Hard Drive. We just can't be sure.

Hyperlink – A link to another website that is just a bit too excited for its own good.

IP address – Your IP (Internet Protocol) is the unique address provided by your ISP (Internet Service Provider), which you learn about if you take ICT.

iTunes – Help you breathe more easily. This is the programme that drives iPods and is constantly being fiddled with by Apple, so much so, that every five minutes it wants to update to the latest version. Like some annoying child who is always asking for their friend to come round.

Java – Programming language discovered on the island next to Sumatra.

JPEG – A compressed photo file that professional photographers turn their noses up at and tell you that a tif is much better. However, when shown both on screen and asked to pick out which is which, they can't tell the difference. Basically, it throws some information away when it compresses the file, but it's hard to know where it took it from.

Keylogger – A programme that spies on your computer by recording which keystrokes you press and sending that information to some shifty little no-good.

Mac – A range of computers beloved by creative people because they're easy to use and they don't have to pay for them themselves. When they have to shell out their own hard cash on a computer, that's not work-related, they'll buy a PC.

Malware – A range of leisure clothes designed for Malcolms everywhere.

Megabyte – One million bytes.

Megahertz – One million cycles per second.

Megapixel – One million pixels.

Megaphone – Used on sports day by a million gym teachers.

Memory Stick – Developed in Silicon Valley at a cost of $98m by the Sony Corporation. It's a stick you hold if you want to remember.

Meta Data – Other data that's not the real data – like data about the data.

Motherboard – The main circuit board of the computer, which all the other major components slot into. If you have to replace it, it's a real mother.

MP3 – Digital music format created by nerds, so you don't have to worry about tape cassettes getting jammed in your Walkman any more.

MPEG – JPEG is a shortened version of "Joint Picture Experts Group", which developed that format. Insert the word "moving" for "joint" and you have MPEG for video files. Graham Norton loves them.

Multiplatform – Works equally badly on PC or Mac.

Nybble – Whereas a byte is made up of eight bits, a nybble is four bits (half a byte). "A nybble is half a byte." Don't you just love those crazy geek guys? When they kick back there's no stopping them.

Packet – Believe it or not, your computer receives information as lots of little packets of data. Each packet contains the IP of its origin and destination, and information that connects it to other packets being sent. If you sign up for Amazon's credit card you can get those packets two days earlier.

Phishing – Phishing is scammers fishing for personal data. They often appear as emails from badly spelt UK banks such as HSCB, Barklays and Lloids. Never click the links in these emails.

Pixel – Photo unit used by fairies.

PlayStation – The reason your child will under-achieve at GCSE and A-level.

Plug-in – A small bit of software that will add extra functionality to something you've already got.

PNG – More like a GIF than a PDF or TIF. It stands for Portable Network Graphic. It also sounds like the code for the international airport at Penang.

Processor – The computer chip that is the "engine room" of your home PC. A dual-core processor is better than a single-core processor. A quad core is better; hard core is what you put under drives. Not disk drives.

Raster – Most images you see on screen are raster images, which are made up of a grid of pixels. Named for Bob Marley in 1974 by a post-graduate science student at UCLA, California.

Recycle Bin – Temporary home for a lot of computer files. On average one in 12 items that is put into the recycle bin gets taken out again.

Router – A device that restores peace in your household when everyone demands their own Internet connection and you need to split it into four.

SCSI – Small Computer Serial Interface, generally pronounced "scuzzy". An old-school connector, the size of a small family saloon car.

SIM – First part of the phrase SIM Card. The tiny element you really want to save when your phone goes "plop" into the bath.

Smartphones – Expensive phone with many features you will never use. Or it'll break after 14 months like my son's Apple 3g and they'll refuse to repair it.

Soundcard – A really good card.

Spider – A programme that roams over the Web (those crazy computer nerds with their arachnid references again) looking for websites to snare, index and inject with poison.

Steve Jobs – The kind of jobs that really suit blokes named Steve.

Telnet – A dedicated Ethernet that links people called Terry.

Unfriend – The act of removing someone from your list of friends on a social networking site. Also known as Defriending. When you make up again, you refriend. If it's never going to work they are imfriendable.

USB – Universal Serial Bus. Sometimes known as the USB2, though like MP1 and MP2 players, nobody ever talks about USB1.

VFAT – Virtual File Allocation Table, or the person you might be sitting next to on the flight to Atlanta.

Wi-Fi – A system that drives your wife to distraction as she roams the house clutching her laptop looking for a connection that was strong in one place on Monday morning but has disappeared entirely by Tuesday.

Wizard – A system that guides you through the installation of a computer programme by hammering the Next key till you get to Finished.

Xbox 360 – See PlayStation.

Yottabyte – Along with a Yobibyte, it is the largest measurement of bytes so far devised. The Yotta is 1,000,000,000,000,000,000,000,000 bytes rounded down from the exact amount, which is the Yobi.

Zebibytes – A piffling 1,000 times less than a Yotta. Call that memory? That's just a casual reminiscence.

THE GRUMPY GARDENER'S HANDBOOK

Ivor Grump

The Grumpy Golfer's Handbook is a compilation of all things frustrating about maintaining the average domestic garden. Grump's attempts to improve his "extra room outdoors" are thwarted at every turn. His lawn develops alopecia, his fruit trees are shunned by all pollinating insects, his veg is a big hit with slugs and his Indian sandstone patio becomes an ingenious sunken garden. All in all, another great book for grumps.

£9.99 • Hardback • 9781907554247

THE GRUMPY DRIVER'S HANDBOOK

Ivor Grump

The Grumpy Driver's Handbook is a celebration of all that is miserable and tedious on the road. Driving brings out the worst in even the most mild mannered individual and so a book on the worst habits in motoring and the 'joys' of car ownership is the natural gift for the career grump. Spurred on by endless roadworks, coned-off lanes, BMW drivers, white van men, speed cameras, lunatic cyclists, rude taxi drivers and kamikazi motorcyclists, the grump has an ocean of opportunity for expression.

£9.99 • Hardback • 9781906032791

ONE GRUMP OR TWO

Arthur Grump

All you want is a decent cup of tea. But oh no, modern Britain doesn't want to give you that. It wants to sell you a fancy coffee in a mug the size of a popcorn bucket, complete with double cream, chocolate sprinkles, and no change from a five-pound note. And that's just for starters. Everywhere you look, modern life has turned common sense completely on its head.

One Grump or Two is for everyone who has ever found Great Britain is starting to grate, and dreams of a world where common sense prevails and the simple things in life remain simple.

£9.99 • Hardback • 9781906032531

THE GRUMPY GOLFER'S HANDBOOK

Ivor Grump

Following in the curmudgeonly footsteps of *One Grump or Two, The Grumpy Golfer's Handbook* is a compilation of all things miserable about playing golf – and there is lots to choose from.

Mark Twain famously said, "golf is a good walk spoiled," but actually it's a lot worse than that. Golf can be a good life spoiled after you become enraged with the behaviour of a Stableford competitor and bury a sand wedge in a place where it's impossible to get relief. Golf, at its worst, is frustrating, tedious and prone to making one feel like throwing your clubs out of the bag. If golf makes you *that* grumpy, this book is for you!

£9.99 • Hardback • 9781906032975